THE LILY ADVENTURES™

SUSPICIOUS IDENTITY

LOIS GLADYS LEPPARD

MOORINGS

NASHVILLE, TENNESSEE

A DIVISION OF THE BALLANTINE PUBLISHING GROUP,
RANDOM HOUSE, INC.

The Lily Adventures™
SUSPICIOUS IDENTITY

Copyright © 1995 by Lois Gladys Leppard

Library of Congress Catalog Card Number: 95-81580

First Edition: November 1995

10   9   8   7   6   5   4   3   2   1

For a very special sister—
Margaret Louise Leppard Langer,
"Little Polly,"
with love always

Seek, and ye shall find.

—Matthew 7:7 KJV

Contents

Chapter One
The Letter

Lily pushed open the door to the attic and walked straight into a huge cobweb. She backed out onto the landing at the top of the steps and tore off her apron. Wiping her face and hands, she shivered as she kept a watch out for any spiders. There was nothing she was more afraid of than those crawly insects.

Thank goodness she had put an old dust cap over her hair. Otherwise her blonde tresses might have had to be washed immediately. She bent to wipe off her shoes just in case the cobwebs had touched them. She stomped her feet.

"Lily, are you all right?" Aunt Ida May called from the second-floor hallway below.

"Oh, Aunt Ida May, there are spiderwebs in the attic," Lily called down to her as she bent over the narrow railing.

Her aunt appeared below as she came up the flight of stairs.

"I know, dear," Aunt Ida May said as she approached Lily. "Somehow we never get around to cleaning up here. Are you all right?"

Lily rolled up her apron and threw it on the floor as she replied, "I think I got it all off." She shook her skirts and shivered again. She could imagine the things crawling all over her.

Ida May looked inside the attic and picked up a broom standing near the doorway. "I always keep this handy to clear the way when I have to come up here for anything. I should have warned you." She began swinging the broom through the air ahead of her as she advanced into the room.

Lily watched as she slowly followed. "It's so dark in here," she said.

"Just you wait right there. I have matches and a lamp right over here," Ida May said. She quickly took a match from a tin box sitting on a small table beside an oil lamp, removed the glass shade, struck the match on the wall, and touched it to the wick. The lamp flared into light and she replaced the glass shade.

The lamp enabled Lily to see around the room. She spied two windows with closed shutters on the far side. "Could I just open those shutters? That would help us to see," Lily said.

"You stay right where you are. I'll do it. There may be some creatures between here and there, and I'm not afraid of them simply because I am bigger than they are," Aunt Ida May said with a little laugh as she made her way through a jumble of boxes, trunks, and furniture.

When Ida May pulled open the shutters and pushed up the windows, light and air poured into the dark, smelly place.

"Oh, what a relief!" Lily said with a big smile.

Her aunt walked back across the room. "Now what can I do to help you?" the old lady asked.

"I don't really know," Lily said as she glanced around. She looked at her furniture, trunks, and other belongings that had been moved here from her father's house. "I thought while Violet is in school now I ought to see if I can make some order out of all this mess. We moved in such a hurry I don't even know where everything is."

"Just take your time, dear," Aunt Ida May told her. "I'll stay right here and you just let me know when I can help." She brushed the dust from a rocking chair with the broom and sat down.

Lily walked around and came to a stop at the pile of furnishings from her father's office. "I suppose I should get all of Papa's papers in some kind of order and keep them in an accessible place," she remarked as she paused by his desk.

"Don't you think you ought to find all your sewing stuff first if you're going to try your hand at making clothes for other people?" Aunt Ida May asked, indicating Lily's sewing machine in the corner. "I'm sure your Aunt Janie Belle won't mind if you take over what used to be the maid's room down behind the pantry for your own sewing room. And we can get Logan and Roy to move the sewing machine down there."

Logan Garrett had been overseer on her father's farm since before sixteen-year-old Lily Masterson was born. Her dear papa's recent death had brought unwanted changes. Her home had been sold, and she and her six-year-old sister, Violet, had nowhere to live.

Her father's sister, Janie Belle, and her husband, Aaron Woods, had taken them into their huge house. Aunt Ida May, Janie Belle's spinster sister, also lived there.

And Roy was foreman for their neighbor, Ossie Creighton, who was like an older brother to Lily.

"But what does Aunt Janie Belle use the room for now?" Lily asked.

"It's empty, dear," Ida May said. "Aggie used to live in

with us when she worked here. Don't you remember? And then when she got married a while back, she set up her own quarters with her husband in town."

"Oh, yes, I remember. I had just forgotten," Lily answered as she looked across the room at the sewing machine. "I suppose it would be better to set up the sewing room first. I might be able to get some work to do."

"I'm sure you'll be able to get something, if it's nothing but hemming skirts or pants. Then you can gradually work yourself into something better," her aunt told her.

Lily walked over to Aunt Ida May. She picked up the broom and swept off the top of a wooden box sitting nearby. "I'm dirty already," she said as she sat down on the box. "A little more won't hurt. Aunt Ida May, I have so many problems I need to solve."

"I know, child, but you don't have to rush into anything right now. You have a home here with your Aunt Janie Belle and me," her aunt said as she reached to squeeze Lily's hand.

"But I can't stay here forever," Lily protested. "It just wouldn't be right for me not to earn my own keep, and Violet is my little sister, so I have to provide a home for her somehow. I do believe I can make a living sewing for other people, but it's going to take a long, long time to do that. I only have the money Logan got for the timber he cut off my father's farm when we had to move, and that isn't very much."

"Don't forget, dear, you have money coming from the family of that man on the ship who was drowned on your way home from England. Every little bit helps," Aunt Ida May reminded her.

Lily pushed back a stray lock of hair under the dust cap and said, "I just don't feel right about accepting that

4

money, somehow. Those people live in Europe, and I don't even know them."

"But you helped identify and capture the man who killed Mr. Ibson, and his family is grateful for that," her aunt told her. "Besides, the captain said the people could well afford to pay a reward. So take the money when it comes and be thankful that you not only helped the family but that it comes at a time when you need it."

Lily changed the subject. "And I need to solve the mystery of my own father's death," she said as tears began to blur her blue eyes. "I've got to catch up with that sheriff and talk to him. Like you, I don't believe my father was killed by a horse. And whoever did it is running around scot-free."

"It may take time, dear, but we'll eventually find the answers to everything," Aunt Ida May assured her.

"And then there's my home the tax people took away from me," Lily said. "I don't believe my father owed any back taxes. You know, there seems to be some kind of conspiracy going against me. And, Aunt Ida May, if Wilbur's father was in such a hurry to buy our property from the tax people, why hasn't he moved into the house yet?"

"Evidently Mr. Whitaker has money and already owns a nice home in town, so I suppose he is in no hurry to move. Or maybe he plans on renting out your house or just farming the land or something. Who knows what's in the heads of these Yankees who come down here with money to burn?" Aunt Ida May said.

Lily got up and began walking around the attic room. "He said he would sell it back to me—when I get the money," she said in an angry voice. "Well, he probably thinks I'll never be able to get my hands on enough money, but he just doesn't know me. I'll get it somehow if it takes me ten years. I'll get my property back." She stopped in front of her aunt. "Yes, let's get that sewing room set up downstairs. The sooner the better." She stretched up to her full five feet and five inches.

Aunt Ida May stood up. "You go ahead and find your needles and thread and things," she said. "I'll go down and speak to your Aunt Janie Belle about the room. I'm sure it'll be all right to use it, but since this is not my own house, I'd better clear it with her first."

"Yes, I don't want to get on the wrong side of Aunt Janie Belle," Lily agreed. "As soon as I locate my supplies, I'll be down—if you're not back up here by then."

Ida May left the room and went on back down the stairs. Lily looked around and tried to remember where she had packed her sewing things. Everything had happened so fast, she still felt as though she were in a daze.

"Oh, Papa, I need you!" she whispered to herself as she looked across the room at his desk. She walked over to it and ran her hand across the top.

As much as she had loved her father, she knew she had to go on living. And in order to do that she needed to start sewing for other people and try to make a living at it. She noticed the big drawer was slightly open, so she bent to push it shut. But it wouldn't close all the way. She pulled it out most of the way and stooped down to straighten the mess of papers in it. When she had them all nice and neat, she pushed the drawer shut. To her surprise it still didn't close tightly.

"Well!" Lily said to herself as she kept pushing the drawer in and out without being able to shut it all the way. She quickly removed the papers from the drawer and lined them up on the floor. Finally she had the drawer light enough to get it all the way out so she could look behind it.

"Well!" Lily exclaimed when she found a whole stack of papers that had fallen inside the desk behind the drawer.

She hurriedly pulled them out and placed them next to the others. Lifting the heavy drawer, she inserted it back into the desk. "Aha!" she said as she pushed it until it was finally closed all the way.

"Now I can fill it back up," she murmured to herself. She began replacing the papers in the drawer, but the contents became too tight to let her tuck in the papers she had found behind the drawer. As she held the stack in her hands she remembered that this was the desk drawer Logan had forced open for her because she had not been able to find her father's keys. She had examined the contents and found bills, paid and unpaid. Now as she glanced down at the stack in her hands, she noticed a thin envelope sealed and marked "Personal and Confidential" in her father's large, scrawled handwriting.

"And what is this?" Lily asked herself as she sat down on a dusty chair nearby and broke the envelope open. She pulled out two sheets of white paper, then gasped when she unfolded them and recognized her mother's handwriting. Her mother had died that summer after years of being an invalid.

" 'My Dearest Husband, Charles,' " Lily read aloud to herself. Her voice trembled as she remembered how her mother always called her father *Charles*. To everyone else he had been Charlie, but she insisted on Charles.

Wiping a tear that was blurring her vision, she continued, " 'I am putting this in writing so that when our darling Lily is grown and ready to marry she can read this for herself. It is my wish that Lily receive all my jewelry at that time if I have left this earth and cannot give it to her myself.' "

Lily paused to think about that. Her jewelry? She didn't know her mother had any jewelry.

" 'You know where to find all my personal belongings of

any value. Please explain to Lily that some of the pieces have been passed down for four generations in my family. I don't know what the monetary value would be, but I have always treasured the jewelry for sentimental reasons and I hope she will, too. However, I would not want her to hesitate one moment if it is absolutely necessary to part with any or all of it.' "

Lily paused again to frown. This was all a mystery to her. And her dear father was not here to explain it to her.

She wiped her eyes again and continued, " 'As for our dear baby, Violet, you know I have already provided for her future, and you alone know the details of that.' "

"Oh, Papa! I don't have anybody to ask about all this," Lily sobbed to herself. "What can I do? If only you had explained to me about this letter!"

Lily bent her head and wept into her hands as the letter fluttered to the floor. "Mama, if only you had talked to me instead of writing it all out for Papa! I realize you had no idea Papa would leave us so soon after you, but I was old enough to be told. What good is this letter now?"

She dried her face on her rumpled skirt and picked up the two sheets of the letter from the dusty floor. As she held the second page with her trembling hands, she finished reading, " 'I love my children with all my heart and hope they will grow up to make you proud of them. As for you, my Charles, there are no words that describe my love for you. May we all be together in the hereafter, Signed, Victoria Sheffield Masters, this 35th anniversary of my birth, 1900.' "

Lily heard Aunt Ida May calling to her as she came up the steps. "Lily, Lily! Have you found everything?"

Lily quickly folded the letter into the envelope and stashed it in the deep pocket of her skirt as she rose to her feet. This was too personal to share with anyone right now.

She loved Aunt Ida May and was grateful for her help and advice, but she wanted to think privately about what her mother had written for a while at least.

"No, Aunt Ida May, not yet," Lily said quietly as she began looking for a place to put the stack of papers that wouldn't fit in the desk drawer. But everything she opened seemed to be chock full. She heard steps behind her and turned around.

"Your Aunt Janie Belle says it will be fine with her if you wish to use the maid's room for your sewing," Aunt Ida May said as she appeared in the doorway. "In fact, she said she might be able to get some work for you from some of her friends."

Lily stopped to look at her. Ida May was fifty years old, young compared to her sister Janie Belle who was seventy. Lily had always thought of Ida May as pretty, with all that dark curly hair and brown eyes, even though she wore black all the time. And Lily had learned only recently the reason for the black attire. Ida May had lost the love of her life when he died a few days before they were to be married, and this information had caused Lily to love her even more.

"Thank you for asking her," Lily said, still holding the stack of papers. "I got sidetracked here, opening drawers and things. These papers fell out of Papa's desk when I opened the drawer, and I haven't found room to stick them anyplace." She began opening the drawers of a bureau. The bottom drawer was half empty. She quickly added the papers, shut the drawer, and turned around to look for her sewing basket. "I don't remember packing my needles and things, so the people who helped us probably did."

"Well now, let's see," Aunt Ida May said as she looked around the attic. "Seems like I remember someone putting that kind of stuff in a trunk. Remember, your trunks had been unpacked and were empty after you all came home from your Aunt Emma's in England?"

"You're right, and there's one of the trunks right over there," Lily said, weaving her way through the jumble to the trunk she had traveled with to England and back. She tried the lid and found she could open it. "Thank goodness it wasn't locked. I don't even know where my keys are." She lifted the lid and bent to look inside.

Ida May had come to her side. "Let's take out the tray, dear," she said. "I believe I remember Aggie putting your things in here."

As they removed the tray, Lily spotted her sewing basket, unused material, and everything that had been stacked on shelves in the kitchen by the sewing machine. "Here they are," Lily said. She started to lift out the sewing basket and then added, "It would be better if I just leave everything in here and get Logan and Roy to move the trunk down to the empty room. That way I won't have everything scattered after I carry it down the steps."

"Then let's go down to the room and measure for some window curtains," her aunt said as they replaced the tray. "I'll make them for you. I have enough material left from the ones I made for the little bedroom downstairs. It's a beautiful light yellow voile and it'll make the room a bright cheery place to work." She turned to leave the attic.

Lily quickly closed the trunk lid and followed her aunt down the steps. Ida May led the way to the empty room, and Lily was glad to see it was on a corner of the house, because it had a window on each side. She also noticed it had its own fireplace.

"This will be nice to work in," Lily said as she walked about the room. "I can put the sewing machine over here by the window and it will be close enough to the fireplace for heat in the winter."

"Yes, and that cold weather is not far off," Aunt Ida May reminded her. "Now let's see what size these windows are." She pulled a tape measure out of her apron pocket and Lily helped to hold it.

"This will only take a minute, and then I'll start work on the curtains," Ida May said as she measured. "I'll make some more-or-less plain, fluffy curtains—nothing formal."

"Whatever you want to make will be fine with me. I appreciate your help, Aunt Ida May," Lily replied, but her mind was on the letter in her pocket. She was not very interested in curtains. Right now she was anxious to get off by herself and read the letter again.

"I'm just glad I can help, even a little bit," her aunt replied, folding up her tape measure. "I'll be working in Janie Belle's sewing room if you need me for anything."

Lily knew Aunt Janie Belle had a large room especially for sewing added to the other side of the house shortly after it was built, years and years before Lily was ever born. She used to get lost in the maze of rooms when she came to visit as a child.

"I'm going back up to the attic while I'm all dirty and go through a few things," Lily told her. "And when I get finished for the day, I'll put out the lamp and close the windows and shutters."

"I'll be on the lookout for Logan and Roy and will let you know if either one of them comes by," Ida May said as they left the room. She turned left down the hallway and Lily went right.

"If they don't show up today, I'll go looking for one of them tomorrow," Lily replied as she went on down the corridor to the back stairs, which went all the way up to the attic.

As soon as Lily got inside the attic room, she pulled the letter out of her pocket and sat down on a box to read it again. *What jewelry was her mother writing about in this letter?* she wondered. *And what did the reference to Violet's future mean? What had she provided for Violet?*

"If only I could understand this letter!" Lily exclaimed as she read and reread it. "Something had been provided for Violet's future, and she will never need it more than she does now. How can I find out what it is? Who might have some information about it?"

She stood up to walk around the room. Suddenly she had an idea—*Logan!* Logan might know something. He had lived on the property as foreman since her grandfather's days and he had been given his own house and a small piece of land when the old man had died.

She stopped to think some more before she looked at the letter in her hand again. "But it says, 'You alone know the details of that.' Only Papa knew," she said aloud to herself. "But Logan is like one of the family, and just maybe Papa confided in him. I need to see him and Roy about moving the trunk downstairs, anyway. I can ask him if he knows anything about this."

Lily finally refolded the letter, placed it back into the envelope, and returned it to her pocket as she walked back over to her father's desk. She would take everything out of it again and go through the papers one by one, just in case there was something else besides bills and farm records.

Chapter Two
Another Letter

"Lily! Lily! It's time to get cleaned up for dinner," Aunt Ida May called from downstairs.

Lily rose hurriedly from the old rocker where she had been sitting with her lap full of Papa's papers and hastily returned them to a huge chest he had kept in his office.

"I'll be right down, Aunt Ida May," she called back as she stuck her head outside the attic door. She ran to close the windows and the shutters, then stopped on the way to blow out the lamp. Closing the door behind her, she went down the narrow steps lighted by the sunlight coming through the window at the landing. "How did it get to be noontime so fast?" she asked herself.

Ida May was waiting for her in the hallway. "I thought you'd like to wash and change clothes before we eat. Aggie will be putting dinner on the table in about ten minutes," her aunt explained.

"Oh, thank you for giving me time, Aunt Ida May. I'm a disgraceful mess and I sure do have to clean up before I can go to the table. And all that dirty work in the attic has to be finished later. I worked on Papa's papers and still didn't get finished," Lily told her.

"All that stuff is not going to run away, dear, so you just work on it when you feel like it," Aunt Ida May replied. "Now, I'll see you in the dining room." She started down the corridor.

"I'll be right there," Lily called to her as she hurried in the other direction to her bedroom.

When Lily stepped inside her bedroom, she took her mother's letter out of her pocket, then quickly removed her dirty clothes and piled them in a corner with plans to wash them later. Finally, she went to the bathroom across the hall to wash up.

Lily felt dirty, and she was glad for the electric water pump that brought water to the kitchen and bathrooms in Janie Belle's mansion, just like at Lily's father's home. But like most of the houses in the community, neither Janie Belle nor her father had wired their homes for electric lights.

Lily was shocked at the image reflected in the mirror over the lavatory.

"Oh, my goodness!" she exclaimed as she hastily wet a washcloth and began scrubbing her face and hands. "How did I get so dirty?"

After she dried on a clean towel, she pulled the dust cap off and was thankful to see that her hair was not dirtied. She quickly brushed stray tendrils of blonde hair back into place and tightened her tortoise shell hairpins. Then she went back to her room and dressed. She put the letter in the pocket of her clean dress.

She got downstairs just as Aunt Janie Belle, Uncle Aaron, and Aunt Ida May were going into the dining room. They sat down at the long table, and Aggie served the food.

"I do hope Violet is getting enough to eat at noontime," Lily said as she took some of the beans. "She's such a hearty eater, and that food she takes in her pail to school every day really doesn't seem like enough for her."

"Nonsense, Lily. You worry too much about that child," Aunt Janie Belle said as she put butter on her cornbread. "You went through the same system when you were growing up in school, and I don't believe you were ever hungry. Besides, you know perfectly well she'll be in the kitchen begging Aggie for cake and milk when she comes home."

"I just wish they let out earlier than three o'clock in the afternoon," Lily said.

"Remember that one teacher has to take time with each age group separately, and I think she does well to finish that early," Uncle Aaron reminded her.

"I'm making pretty good progress on your curtains for the sewing room," Aunt Ida May told Lily. "They'll probably be ready to hang tomorrow."

"Thank you, Aunt Ida May. And Aunt Janie Belle, I want to thank you for letting me use the room for my sewing. I don't know whether I'll be able to make much money sewing for other people, but then I won't know until I try," Lily said.

"That's right. All you have to do is begin," Aunt Janie Belle said as she shifted her hefty weight in the chair. "I'll see what I can do to round up some work for you from some of our acquaintances."

"Thank you," Lily said. "Has Logan been by today? Or Roy? I need them to move a trunk downstairs for me."

"No, I imagine Ossie is keeping Roy pretty busy after Ossie being gone so long to England. And Logan is working his own land, but he'll probably show up tonight."

"Yes, he's always asking if there's anything he can do for us," Lily said as she ate her food. "I really feel bad about ever asking him to do anything, since he doesn't work for us anymore."

"Oh, you hush now, child," Aunt Ida May said. "You know Logan feels like he's one of the family. He loves doing things for you."

"Well, I hope someday I'll be able to reward him somehow," Lily said. "I don't know how I'll do it, but someday I'll have my house and land back and will hire him to oversee everything for me, like he did for Papa."

"Lily, you might as well forget about these pipe dreams. That man Whitaker is never going to let you have your father's house back, and you know it," Aunt Janie Belle said.

"But, Aunt Janie Belle, he told me he would sell it back to me when I got the money," Lily replied as she set down her coffee cup.

"And did he say how much that would be?" Aunt Janie Belle asked.

"Well, no. But I understood it to be the amount he paid for it," Lily replied.

"Come down to earth! That property is worth a whole lot more than what he paid for it, and he's a *businessman* out to make *money*, so don't plan on getting it back for that much," Aunt Janie Belle said.

Tears sprang into Lily's blue eyes as she made herself realize her aunt was right. Things really did look hopeless. She quickly touched her napkin to her lips as she bowed her head slightly without replying.

"As soon as you're finished eating, dear, I want you to come and look at the curtains, and see if you think they're going to be all right," Ida May said as she frowned at Janie Belle and turned to look at Lily.

"Sure," Lily said, just barely managing to control her voice. She picked up her coffee cup and drank from it.

16

Ida May must have noticed her concern, because she changed the subject to relieve the tension at the table. "I've been thinking, Janie Belle, while things are more or less slack with Aggie's work right now, since we've canned everything we can find, Aggie and I could give the attic a thorough cleaning. It sure needs it. Lily walked smack into a huge cobweb up there this morning," Ida May said to her sister.

"Oh, goodness, yes, if there are spiders up there, please get rid of them," Janie Belle replied, visibly shivering at the mention of spiders.

Lily, listening to the exchange between her aunts, understood Ida May's tactics at once. The mention of the insects was a sure way of gaining Aunt Janie Belle's approval to clean the attic. She glanced at Aunt Ida May and smiled.

"We could also help Lily with anything she wants to retrieve from the attic for her room or Violet's," Ida May continued. "Everything was done in such haste, Lily hasn't been able to locate some things she needs."

Janie Belle looked at her sister with a frown and said, "Ida May, you're a grown woman. You don't have to ask my permission to do anything. This is your home, same as mine."

Ida May smiled at her and said, "Thank you, Janie Belle, you have always been so considerate. I'll talk to Aggie and we'll start in the morning, as soon as breakfast is over with and cleared away."

Janie Belle began pushing her chair back, and Uncle Aaron rose to help her. "Now get on with your curtains or whatever. I must have a little rest, and I have a new book to read," she said as she finally managed to rise from the table.

"Aunt Janie Belle, I have a good many books. When we get things straightened out and find them, you would be welcome to read anything I have," Lily said as she rose. "I have a copy of *Little Women* and also *Little Men* that I've had for a long time. I know you like that kind of book. And I also have the latest book about President McKinley, and lots of other books, too."

"Why, yes, dear, I'd appreciate the opportunity to read them. In fact, I'd like to see anything you might have. I always seem to be running out of reading material."

"As soon as I find my books, I'll bring them down," Lily promised as she followed Ida May from the room.

Ida May led the way to Aunt Janie Belle's sewing room and showed Lily the yellow material already cut and basted. Her aunt picked up one panel and explained, "This will hang full, with lots of gathers, and I'll put a frill across the bottom and up the side."

"They're going to be awfully pretty, Aunt Ida May," Lily replied as she looked at the work her aunt had done. Then she quickly added, "But I know the curtains were an excuse to change the subject at the table."

Ida May looked straight at her as they stood there in the sewing room and said, "Yes, dear, it was. Please don't let anything your Aunt Janie Belle says discourage you. Keep up your faith and determination, and I'm sure you will eventually accomplish whatever you set out to do."

Lily reached to put an arm around the woman. "Thank you, Aunt Ida May. Aunt Janie Belle's remarks just made me realize there is no telling how much Mr. Whitaker will ask for the house and land," she said, and then quickly added, "but whatever it is, I'll get it. I won't give up."

Ida May gave her a squeeze. "Remember the verse 'Seek, and you shall find' and you'll find a way," she said as she turned back to the curtains. "Now, I'll get back to work on these so we can get you in business."

"I think I'll walk down to the road and see if there's any

mail in the box," Lily told her. "Then I'll probably look for my books in the attic."

Ida May glanced at her and said, "You look awfully pretty and clean to go back up in that dirty place. Why don't you wait until I get Aggie started cleaning things up?"

Lily looked down at her neat calico dress and said, "I'll put on a big apron. I won't get all dirty again." She laughed and continued, "Now that you've knocked the spiders out of the way, I have a clear path to my trunks."

"When we do catch up with Logan, we'll also need help with hanging these curtains," Ida May reminded her as she sat down at the sewing machine.

"All right, if he doesn't come by today, I'll ride over early in the morning and try to catch him before he gets out and is gone for the day," Lily said as she left the room.

She found her way out of the house and strolled down to the road. Violet's white puppy kept running ahead and her white kitten followed around her ankles. It did no good to try to make them go back. They insisted on going with her.

"I don't want you coming out to the road," Lily told the puppy as she picked him up, spanked his behind, set him down in the direction of the house, and said, "Now get back home." She stomped her feet at him and the kitten. He just stood there wagging his tail. The kitten ran for the bushes along the way and then stopped to watch. "Oh, you're hopeless!" Lily said with a little laugh as she went on her way while the two animals stayed a little ways behind her.

When Lily reached the mailbox, she opened the door and found one letter inside. It was for her—from Aunt Emma Sheffield, her mother's sister she and Violet had visited that summer in England.

"At last!" Lily said with a big sigh as she stood there and

broke the seal on the envelope. She had written her aunt about her father's death and the loss of their property quite a while ago.

"My Dear Lily," she read to herself from the single sheet inside. "I was certainly shocked to hear the news about your father. You and Violet must come back to me at once. You have a home here. I just wish you had not made that long journey back to United States and now have to make it all over again to return here. From what you told me about your property, I would agree there is a rotter involved, but I have no hope that you can ever open things up to reveal the truth. Let me know at once when to expect you and Violet, and I will get things ready. Remember you have a home here. With love to you both, Aunt Emma."

Lily slowly folded the one sheet of tinted paper, replaced it in the envelope, and reached to put it in her pocket. Her hand made contact with the letter written by her mother. She pulled it out, looked at the envelope a moment, and then slipped both letters inside.

"Aunt Emma, thank you and I love you, but no," Lily said to herself as she walked back down the driveway to the house. The two little animals followed.

Lily returned to the sewing room to share the news with Aunt Ida May.

"It's awfully kind of her to offer Violet and me a home, but I could never live in England," Lily said. "My people are all here. I always wondered how my mother could go off to another country and live."

"Well, in your mother's case, dear, it was love," Ida May said, looking up from the sewing machine where she had stopped work on the curtains. "Your mother came to this country with some friends to visit their relatives here. She met your father and decided to stay. I suppose you know all that."

"She used to talk to me about it," Lily said with a far-away look in her eyes. "She stayed here and never even went back to visit her family in England. Of course Aunt Emma came here one summer when I was small, but she was the only one. When we went to England this past summer, Aunt Emma told us the other relatives had all died."

"Real love can be strong enough to change your life, dear," Aunt Ida May said. "I was willing to give up my home and my father for the one I loved, but of course you know I lost him through that accident before our wedding day."

"It's hard for me to realize what it must be like to love someone that much," Lily said as she sat on a stool nearby. "I've always loved my family and would never give them up for anything, but that's different from the kind of love you're talking about. For some reason it scares me to think that might happen to me someday if I met a true love. I don't think I could ever love someone that much."

"There's nothing you can do about it, dear," Aunt Ida May told her as she smiled. "If you ever truly fall in love, you'll understand, and you probably will someday meet someone you would give up everything for."

Lily shivered at the very thought of something like that taking over her life. She stood up and walked around the room.

"I don't want to fall in love," she said. She stopped and turned back to look at Ida May. She had shared her life secrets with Lily, and now Lily decided to share her secret with Ida May.

"What is it, dear?" Ida May asked as Lily stooped down beside her.

"Aunt Ida May, I have already received a proposal of

marriage and have not accepted it," Lily began. She paused.

"Yes, I know, child," Aunt Ida May said with a big smile. "Anyone could see how much Ossie loves you, except you yourself."

Lily stood up and looked down at her. "But how could you tell? He asked me to marry him so Violet and I could have a place to live and someone to take care of us."

"But that night on your front porch," Ida May said, "after I went into the house, he told you he loved you, didn't he?"

"Well, yes, he did, but I'm not sure he meant it," Lily said. "He was worried about what we would do when our home was taken away from us for taxes."

"Oh, Lily, how can you not see that Ossie truly loves you?" Ida May asked.

Lily shrugged her shoulders and said, "I'm not sure. Anyway, I don't love him in that way, to marry him, that is. But I do love him like a big brother."

"Maybe you'll understand someday," Ida May said.

Lily wanted to end the conversation, so she said, "Well, anyhow, I'm going back up to the attic and look for my books now. If you see Violet when she comes home from school, would you please tell her where I am?"

"Of course, dear," Ida May said as she began sewing again.

Lily stopped by her room and put on a large apron, then tied a scarf around her head.

As she opened the attic door, she picked up the broom and waved it ahead of her as she hurried forward to open the windows. The sunshine was bright enough on that side of the house now that she didn't light the lamp. Then she sat down in the chair she had dusted off that morning and pulled both the letters from her pocket. She held the envelopes side by side without opening them.

"My mother and her sister," she said to herself. "I wonder if I ought to mention to Aunt Emma this letter my mother wrote."

No, somehow her mother's letter was too private to share. She thought about how young and pretty her mother had been before her illness ruined her health. She thought about how much older and simpler Aunt Emma was. Aunt Emma had never married and was all alone over there in England, but Lily knew she had lots of friends because someone was always visiting when she and Violet were there. *Two sisters*, Lily thought, *the only children in their family, separated all these years by the ocean. How could they have stayed apart?* She would never leave her little sister—under any circumstances.

Lily's father's people seemed altogether different from her mother's, and they felt more like family. They all lived in the same community and visited back and forth almost every day. And her father's two surviving sisters were even living in the same house.

Lily shook her head to clear out such thoughts, put the letters back in her pocket as she stood up, and said, "This is not getting anything done."

She didn't bother with her father's papers this time, because that was going to be a time-consuming task to get them all in order. Instead she began searching for her books. Everything had been packed in such a hurry with so many people helping that she found books stuffed into different boxes and even in some of the drawers of the bureau that had been in their guest room.

"Aha!" she said aloud as she finally located the three books she had mentioned to Aunt Janie Belle. Some of

Violet's books were packed with them, and just as she pulled them out, Violet came to the door of the attic.

"Lily, are you in here?" the child asked from the doorway.

Lily stood up from where she had been stooping to look into drawers and said, "Yes, dear, I'm over here, but please be careful and don't touch anything because everything is so dirty."

Six-year-old Violet worked her way through the jumble to Lily. She spotted her books on top of the bureau.

"My books!" she exclaimed. "Can I take these down to my room, Lily?"

"Of course, dear, I was just going to bring them down myself," Lily said. Then she remembered the mail from Aunt Emma, "By the way, we got a letter from Aunt Emma today." She pulled the letter out of her pocket to show her little sister.

Violet reached for it; Lily let her have it. The child pulled the letter out of the envelope and looked it over, then handed it back to Lily. "What does it say? I can't read it. I go to school now, but I haven't learned to read letters yet."

"But you'll be able to before long if you study real hard," Lily said, taking the letter. She read the entire contents to Violet, who stood listening carefully.

"Lily, Aunt Emma said we have a home there. Let's go over there," Violet said.

"But we have a home here right now, dear," Lily explained. "You wouldn't want to go on that long journey across the ocean again, would you?"

"No, Lily, we do not have a home here," Violet protested as she flipped back her long blonde hair. Tears sprang into her blue eyes as she added, "Aunt Janie Belle just now told me not to bring my puppy in the house anymore."

Lily caught her breath. It *was* happening. Aunt Janie Belle was beginning to get strict with Violet and Lily didn't know how to handle it.

"So my puppy does not have a home if he can't come in the house," Violet added. "And Aunt Emma let him come in her house when we lived there."

"Well, you see, it's like this, dear. Some people let puppies come in the house and some people don't. And since it's Aunt Janie Belle's house, we have to do whatever she says. She's just worried that your puppy might do some damage," Lily tried to explain.

"But he's little. He won't hurt her house," Violet said, tears beginning to stream down her cheeks.

Lily quickly bent and held her in her arms. "But we have to let her have the say-so about that," Lily said. "Besides, I think your puppy prefers staying outdoors. Now, where is your kitten?"

"Oh, he's outside, too," Violet said tearfully as she wiped her eyes. "Since my puppy couldn't come in the house, I left my kitten out there to keep him company."

Lily smiled and tried to change the subject. "Violet, you still haven't decided on a name for that puppy. He just has to have a name. Why don't you go back outside with him and make a decision about a name? And that kitten will have to have a name, too. Since Aunt Janie Belle gave him to you, you should ask her opinion of a name for the kitten."

Violet pulled away from her. "Why does Aunt Janie Belle tell me what to do?" she asked. "Let's go to Aunt Emma. She said we have a home there, and I suppose it would be a real home because she likes my puppy."

Lily stood up and looked down at her little sister. "Violet, we'd better get some things straight right now," she said. "This is Aunt Janie Belle's house, and as long as she is nice enough to let us live here, we have to do whatever she says. We didn't have any other place to go, and she let us move in here."

"Let's go back to our house then, Lily," Violet said. "It's still empty. Ossie said so. I saw him on the way home from school. Let's go live next door to him again."

"Violet, there are some things I just can't explain to you because you're too young to understand, but we don't own our house anymore," Lily said, becoming impatient with the child. "Someday we'll get enough money to buy it back, and then we can move back into it. But right now we have to live with Aunt Janie Belle. Now you take your books here down to your room and then go on outside and play with your puppy. He's been waiting all day for you to come home from school and play with him."

"He has?" Violet said, looking up at her in surprise.

"Yes, he follows me around when I go outside because you have been gone," Lily told her. "You go ahead now, and I'll be down in a little while."

Violet scooped up the books that belonged to her and turned to leave the room. She stopped at the doorway, looked back, and said, "Just don't forget, Lily, Aunt Emma said we had a home over there."

"Yes, I know," Lily replied as she bent to open a box, and Violet went on out of the room.

"I just hope she doesn't do something to cause Aunt Janie Belle to get angry with us," Lily said to herself as she pulled books out of the box.

She needed to settle down and start making some money. If she worked hard enough and got enough business, she'd be able to move out somewhere else. But where, she did not know. It would take a long time to get her home back.

Chapter Three
Questions Without Answers

L ily made several trips down the stairs as she carried her books to her room. She moved the huge family Bible to the night table by her bed and lined the books up across the long bureau until she could get a bookcase brought from the attic. Laying the three books for Aunt Janie Belle on her bed, Lily decided to look into Violet's room and see what she had done with her books.

"Well!" Lily said with a big smile as she looked through the doorway and saw that her little sister had placed them in a neat pile on the desk in the corner. Lily had allowed her to take the desk from their mother's furniture to use for her schoolwork.

Lily returned to her own room, and just as she stepped inside, Violet came running up the stairs calling her, "Lily! Lily!"

"I'm here," Lily replied as she looked out into the hallway.

"Aunt Ida May says to tell you Logan is downstairs," Violet told her, then she turned and went back downstairs.

Lily took off her apron and scarf, threw them on a chair, and transferred the letters to her skirt pocket. She picked up the books for Aunt Janie Belle and hurried after her. She wanted to ask Logan about her parents' business affairs.

She found everyone sitting in the kitchen where the huge iron cookstove warmed the room. Violet was playing with the puppy and kitten in a corner, and Lily wondered if Aunt Janie Belle noticed.

"Oh, Logan, I'm so glad you came by," Lily said as she paused to hand the three books to Aunt Janie Belle. "I need a few things moved down from the attic and I was wondering if you and Roy could do it for me."

Logan twisted his broad-brimmed hat in his hands as he looked at her and said, "Course, anything you need done, we'll be more than glad to do it for you. Miss Ida May here already mentioned you're settin' up a sewin' business."

"Thanks, Logan," Lily said as she sat on a stool nearby. She looked at him and laughed as she added, "And anything you might need in the way of sewing, I'll be glad to do free of charge."

"We'll argue about that later," Logan said. "I jes' need a few work clothes patched where they're wearin' out. I reckon you know how to do that."

"Of course, Logan. Remember, I kept Papa's clothes mended," Lily said with a sad smile. "You just bring whatever you have over here and I'll get to work on it."

Logan stood up and smoothed back his thick grey hair. "Well, I must be gettin' along now. I'll see if Roy can come back with me tonight, and we'll move the stuff for you," he said.

"Logan, now you sit right back down," Ida May told him as she stood up. "I'm just afixin' to put supper on the table."

Lily started to join in the invitation, but she realized this was not her house to invite people to supper. She glanced at Aunt Janie Belle and noticed that she was not saying a word.

"Thank you, ma'am, but I'd best be goin'," Logan replied as he started for the back door.

Lily felt bad because when Aunt Ida May had stayed with her and Violet in their house, before they moved in with Aunt Janie Belle, Logan had always accepted her invitation to a meal. He lived alone and seemed to appreciate sitting at their table. Aunt Janie Belle did not seem to be so welcoming to have him eat with them. Uncle Aaron sitting in a rocker next to his wife also remained silent.

"Well then, when you come back, you and Roy plan on having a cup of nice hot coffee with a piece of the cake I baked today," Ida May told him as she walked toward the stove. She looked back at him with a big smile and added, "The cake is chocolate."

Logan smiled back as he started to open the back door. "Sounds like something that jes' can't be turned down. See y'all after while."

Lily hurried to the door after him. "Aunt Ida May, I was just going out to see if Lightnin' is all right," she said. "I haven't seen him today. I'll be right back."

Once outside in the yard, Lily told Logan, "I really wanted to talk to you privately a minute about something. Let's walk down to the fence."

Her horse, Lightnin', was kept in the pasture behind the barn, and when he saw his mistress approaching, he came to greet her.

Lily reached to rub the big animal's head with one hand as she pulled her mother's letter out of her pocket with the other. Then she turned to Logan and showed it to him.

"I found this envelope in Papa's desk," Lily explained as

she held it out. She opened it and took out the letter, "This is something my mother wrote, and I want to read part of it to you."

Logan stood waiting as he listened and watched her.

"I would like to know if you ever knew anything about any jewelry my mother might have owned," Lily said. "She says in here, 'It is my wish that Lily receive all my jewelry.' But I don't remember ever seeing her wear any jewelry. Do you?"

Logan thought for a moment and then he replied, "Seems like I faintly remember seein' your mother wearing jewelry when she first married your papa, but I don't know what it was, seems like some pearls, maybe with what might have been diamonds—earrings, a bracelet, and whatnot. Understand, I'm not sure about it. And I couldn't say whether it was real stuff or not, 'cause I don't know that much about jewelry."

Lily thoughtfully replied, "Pearls? Diamonds? I can't remember any at all. But then I was only ten years old when she became ill and stopped dressing in fancy clothes. And, of course, if she and Papa got dressed up for a party or something, I was too young to be allowed in on it."

"Now, I need to be goin' so I can catch Roy," Logan told her.

"Please wait just a minute more," Lily said as she detained him with her hand on his arm. "Let me read one other thing in this letter. It says, 'As for our dear baby, Violet, you know I have already provided for her future, and you alone know the details of that.' Do you have any idea as to what that means?" She looked up at him anxiously.

"I'm sorry, Miss Lily, but I have no idea what that's all about at all," Logan said. "Sounds to me like she had set aside some money or something for Violet."

"Money?" Lily repeated as she folded the letter, placed it back inside the envelope, and added, "Do you suppose my mother had her own money from somewhere? Like maybe she got money from her relatives in England?"

Logan shook his head and said, "Miss Lily, you got yourself a real mystery and I can't help you 'cause I jes' don't know nothin'. Now, let me be on my way."

Lily followed him up to the driveway to where he had left his horse and asked, "Logan, will you please think about these things, a whole lot, and maybe you'll remember something or other about all this?"

"I'll think about it," Logan agreed as he mounted his horse. "Soon as I can round up Roy I'll be back."

"Thanks," Lily called after him as she put the letter back in her pocket.

She was disappointed because she had been hoping Logan, who had been around the farm every day while her father was living, might remember something. She didn't want to share the letter with anyone else. Besides, her aunts were her father's sisters, and they probably wouldn't have ever known anything about her mother's business.

Keeping her hand on the letter inside her pocket, Lily went back inside the house. Ida May was getting supper ready and Lily helped. As she set the table, she glanced at Aunt Janie Belle and Uncle Aaron sitting over near the window. Both of them were reading, and neither one offered to assist Ida May with supper. Lily was beginning to see how her Aunt Janie Belle took advantage of her sister Ida May. She seemed to expect Ida May to wait on her hand and foot.

Lily helped Aunt Ida May place all the food on the table. Finally Aunt Janie Belle, with Uncle Aaron's assistance, hefted her large frame out of the rocking chair and went to the table.

Lily quietly and quickly motioned to Violet to put the puppy in the box behind the stove, wash her hands, and come to the table. She glanced at Aunt Janie Belle, but the woman didn't seem to notice as Violet obeyed.

As they sat around the table, Lily was trying to figure out some way to ask Aunt Janie Belle questions about her mother. She knew Janie Belle was ten years older than her father and had been living in this house when Charlie and Victoria, her mother, met. Ida May was ten years younger than Charlie and, therefore, would have been a young woman when Lily's parents married.

"Aunt Janie Belle, tell me about my mother," Lily said, looking at her aunt down at the end of the table. "What was she like when she met my father?"

Janie Belle cleared her throat, looked at Lily, and replied, "Well, she was young and pretty. But she wasn't very friendly with anyone I know of, besides your father. Charlie was her world."

"She wasn't?" Lily questioned. She remembered her mother before her illness as being easygoing and pleasant with everyone.

"I hate to say this, but she had those foreign ways about her—hard to get acquainted with and never a real friend with anyone I know of," Janie Belle said as she cut the meat on her plate.

"Oh, really?" Lily said, glancing at Ida May across the table from her.

"Now, Janie Belle, she was friendly with me," Ida May protested. "Of course I was considerably older than she was, so we didn't have much in common, but I was always welcome in your home, Lily."

Lily looked at Aunt Janie Belle and said, "You said she was pretty. Did she have lots of pretty clothes and jewelry?"

Janie Belle frowned as she looked at Ida May and then back to Lily. "I'd say her clothes were expensive and right up to the minute in style, but that was so many years ago when she was able to get dressed up that I can't rightly remember exactly what she wore. The only thing I definitely recall was a pearl necklace she wore over here when she and Charlie came to a social we had. That pearl necklace must have been worth something, because somehow it broke and those pearls rolled all over the room, and she got down on her hands and knees to find them."

"A pearl necklace? And it broke. Did she have it restrung?" Lily asked, remembering what Logan had said about pearls.

Janie Belle struggled to remember as she continued eating and said, "Why, I don't know. I have no idea as to whether she even found all the pearls or not."

"I remember that happening," Ida May said as she laid down her fork. "It was made in two or three strands—three I believe—and it was only one strand that actually broke. She could have worn it again as just two strands if she'd wanted to."

"Was that a long time ago?" Lily asked.

"I believe it was not long after they got married," Janie Belle said. Then she added, "I think she also had some kind of jewelry with colored stones, either rubies or emeralds or something bright like that. But, mind you, this was all when they first got married. Later, when she became ill after Violet was born, I don't remember ever seeing her dressed up again."

"No, but she still had lots of pretty clothes," Ida May said. "Seems like she gave a lot of them to her sister Emma when she came over here to visit. And I know you can remember your aunt coming from England to see your mother, Lily. You were about ten years old then, right after she got so sick. It's a shame she couldn't live to see her daughters grow up and get married."

Lily remembered what her mother had said in her letter about Lily getting married. Everyone seemed to take it for granted that was all a girl had to do, just grow up and get married. Suppose she didn't want to get married? And Violet? Who knew what that child would grow up to want to do?

"Do you suppose she gave Aunt Emma her jewelry, too? I went through most of her things when we packed to move over here and I didn't see any jewelry," Lily said, trying to be casual about the question.

Ida May and Janie Belle looked at each other. Then after a moment Janie Belle replied, "I have no idea. I can't see why your mother would give jewelry to her sister, that is, if it were real jewelry. It should have been saved for you."

"Yes, and I would say those pearls must have been valuable," Ida May added. "Are you sure you've looked into everything that belonged to your mother, dear? Maybe valuable things like jewelry could be in some safe place and not with other things."

"I'll go back to the attic tomorrow while Aggie is cleaning and look again," Lily said, drinking her coffee.

"I want to go, too," Violet said, suddenly making Lily realize her little sister had been awfully quiet at the table. Evidently Violet had been listening to all the conversation.

"You will be in school tomorrow morning while I go up there," Lily reminded her. "But one day soon, after Aggie gets it all cleaned up, I promise you and I will go up there and look everything over."

"Soon," Violet said as she crammed her mouth full of food. "Don't forget."

"I won't forget," Lily said.

And she wouldn't forget. Violet needed to be able to

touch her mother's things to help retain the memory of the woman. And Papa's things, too, Lily was thinking. But there was no danger of Violet forgetting her father. She had been constantly at his heels every time she got a chance. On the other hand, their mother had been ill all of Violet's life, and the child hardly knew her.

After the supper table was cleared, Lily and Ida May went up to the attic to decide what the men should bring down when they came. Violet stayed in the kitchen to play with her puppy and kitten. Aunt Janie Belle and Uncle Aaron went to their room to read by the open fireplace.

When Logan returned with Ossie Creighton's foreman, Roy, Violet brought them up to the attic. She also brought her puppy and kitten. And Lily immediately sent her back downstairs with the animals.

"Violet, you have to take the puppy and kitten back down to the kitchen," Lily told her. "They'll get into everything here and be in the way."

Violet frowned and her blue eyes stared at Lily as she stood there.

"Now, Violet," Lily said firmly. "Take them back now. If you want to come back up by yourself, you may, but no animals in the attic."

Violet drew a big sigh, turned, and left the attic.

Lily turned back to the men who were waiting. "I think the sewing machine ought to go downstairs first. I can place it and see how much space I'll have for other things," she told them. And pointing to her trunk, she added, "And all my sewing equipment is in that trunk, so it needs to go, too."

"Anything you say, Miss Lily," Logan said as he and Roy approached the sewing machine.

"I remember helping bring this thing up the stairs. It's

heavy, but at least this time we'll be going down," Roy remarked as he and Logan grasped the ends.

Lily laughed and said, "And I promise not to ask you to bring it back up the steps."

The steps from the attic to the floor below were narrow and the turn in the landing was sharp. After that the stairway was wide, and the men had no trouble getting the machine to the first floor and into Lily's new sewing room.

"By the window," Lily directed them. "That will give me light, and air in the summer." Logan and Roy set the machine down and returned to the attic.

The men followed her instructions and brought down other pieces of furniture and the trunk. Ida May helped Lily carry small boxes of odds and ends. Soon the room was full, and everything was in place. The four of them stood back and looked at it.

"I believe you've got a real business set up here, Miss Lily," Logan remarked.

"And I want to be one of the first customers," Roy added. "I've got lots of mending that needs to be done."

"Whoa there," Logan said with a laugh. "I'm ahead of you for that kind of stuff. Miss Lily has already promised."

Lily smiled at the two men and said, "Both of you just bring everything you need fixed and I'll get it done in no time." She looked at them mischievously and added, "Now if you both would send your lady friends here to get their dressmaking done, I'd appreciate that, too."

Everyone laughed.

"I'll have to get me a lady friend first," Logan joked.

"And you know my lady friend lives way down in Laurens County and has a houseful of kids to raise after her husband died, and I don't imagine she could afford a dressmaker," Roy replied. "But I will tell my boss man, Ossie, to bring his stuff over, provided you put me ahead of him on your list."

"You see, Lily, you are getting customers before you even get open for business," Ida May said, smiling at everyone.

"Yes, and I may get more than I can handle all of a sudden," Lily said with a little laugh. "Remember, this is a one-woman operation, and you men will have to be patient."

Roy and Logan laughed.

"Don't worry about that, Lily," Aunt Ida May told her. "I plan on helping you get started. Now, let's all go out to the kitchen and get rid of that pot of coffee on the stove and that chocolate cake I made."

"I say amen to that," Logan said.

"I knew I'd get something good that Miss Ida May baked," Roy added.

In the kitchen Lily quickly set down cups, saucers, cake plates, and silverware from the cupboard. Ida May poured the coffee and brought the cake from the pie safe and cut it into large slices.

"Let's eat this stuff before it disappears," Lily told the men as each of them pulled out one of the cane bottom chairs from under the table and sat down.

Just as Ida May was passing the cake around, Lily suddenly missed Violet. She looked around the room. The puppy and the kitten were not there, either.

"Excuse me just a second," Lily said, getting up from the table. "I don't know where Violet and her pets are. I'll be right back."

She hurried up the stairs to Violet's room, which had the door closed. When she quietly pushed it open, she found Violet on the bed, sound asleep, with the puppy on one side and the kitten on the other.

Lily quietly picked up the puppy, placed him in his box in the corner, and moved the kitten enough to pull the covers over Violet. She didn't want to wake her. She could just as well sleep in her clothes for the night. The kitten softly meowed one time and then curled back up beside Violet on top of the cover.

Returning to the kitchen, Lily explained that Violet had gone to sleep and would be furious if she had known they were enjoying chocolate cake without her.

"She doesn't need to eat so late anyway," Lily said, smiling. She looked at Ida May and said, "Violet told me earlier that Aunt Janie Belle had said the animals would no longer be allowed in the house. I'm afraid these animals are going to cause trouble between us and Aunt Janie Belle."

Ida May laughed and said, "Don't you worry about your Aunt Janie Belle. She has probably forgotten by now that she ever gave that order. Besides, Violet had them here in the kitchen before we ate supper. She was playing with them behind the stove, and Janie Belle was sitting here with us and didn't say anything."

"I figured she didn't really notice them," Lily said. "Anyhow, Violet and I have to be on good behavior while we're in someone else's house. Oh, if I can only get a real business going so we can move out on our own somewhere . . ."

The other three were all silent, and Lily could feel their sad looks at her. They had paused in their eating.

"Don't y'all worry about me," Lily said with a nervous laugh. "Violet and I will make it and someday we'll be living back in our own house."

No one spoke.

"I believe there was something crooked about our losing our home and I won't rest until I find out why we lost it," Lily remarked.

"Now, that's the spirit," Ida May said. "Never give up. And the Lord will look after those that help themselves . . ."

"Logan, I want to go back to Greenville and try to catch that sheriff one day soon," Lily said as Ida May filled their cups with more coffee. "I want to have a talk with him about Papa."

"Anytime you want to go, I'll be ready," Logan said, drinking his coffee.

"And if Logan is not available, I'll go with you," Roy added, eating the last of his slice of chocolate cake.

"Thanks. I'll have to get my work set up and things going before I can take the time to go," Lily told them. "And I have to do some sorting in the attic. I want to be sure I know where everything is."

"I'll have the curtains ready to hang tomorrow if one of you men can come back and put them up for us," Ida May said.

"Now hold on a minute. I've already been asked to do that honor," Logan said with a big smile as he looked at Roy.

"Well, next time ask me first," Roy said, laughing. Turning to Lily, he said seriously, "Don't forget, Miss Lily, I'm always available for anything you need done."

"Thanks. I'm glad to know I have such true friends," Lily said.

Lily was wishing her friends could help her solve the mystery of her mother's jewels and the provision for Violet her mother had mentioned in the letter, but Lily knew they couldn't. And the letter was too personal to share with anyone else. She reached to put her hand on the pocket holding the two letters.

"I finally heard from Aunt Emma in England after I wrote her about Papa," Lily said, changing the subject.

"The mail is so slow. She has asked me and Violet to come live with her."

She heard gasps around the table.

Smiling at her friends, she added, "Don't worry. We're not moving to England. That's for sure."

"I hope not," Logan said with a frown.

"And we just wouldn't allow you to go," Ida May said, looking directly at Lily.

"And I'd help hogtie you to keep you from leaving," Roy said with a big laugh.

"I'd like to go back and visit sometime, since Aunt Emma is my mother's sister, but I wouldn't stay long," Lily told them.

Logan pushed back his chair and stood up. Roy followed. "I best be gettin' home so y'all can hit the hay. I thank you, Miss Ida May, for the tasty chocolate cake. They get better every time."

"And I also thank you. I've really enjoyed it," Roy added.

Lily and Ida May rose as the men walked over to the pegs by the back door to get their coats and hats.

"Roy," Lily began and paused.

Roy looked at her and asked, "Yes?"

"Roy, you live right next door to my house," Lily said quickly. "I was just wondering if you'd seen anyone about the yard or in the house."

Roy shook his head and said, "No, not a soul. Ossie remarked on that. He said it looks like Mr. Whitaker would be doing something with the property. And don't tell a soul, but Ossie asked me to keep the yard clean around the house, just for you, he said."

Tears sprang into Lily's blue eyes as she replied, "Sounds like Ossie. I'd hate to see the yard all grown up and in need of cleaning. I thank you."

After the men left, Lily helped Ida May clear off the table.

"Lily, don't you understand? Ossie does love you," Ida May said as she washed the dishes and Lily dried them.

Lily didn't want to talk about it. The fact that Ossie was keeping her yard clean had upset her.

Taking a deep breath, she smiled weakly at her aunt and said, "Aunt Ida May, if I ever fall in love with Ossie or with anyone else, you can be sure you will be the first to know."

Later as she undressed for bed, Lily made plans for the next day. She would help Aggie in the attic and examine everything up there that belonged to her. If there were any jewels belonging to her mother in one of those drawers or boxes, she would find them.

Chapter Four
New Ideas

Aggie had been working for Janie Belle many years, but she was still fast, efficient, and talkative—that is, when Janie Belle was not in the room. Lily had never really been around the woman much and thought she was moody, but then she caught on. Janie Belle didn't allow too much talking on the job, and Aggie didn't have too much that she wanted to say in Janie Belle's presence. But she made up for lost time when she was with someone else.

Ida May led the way up the narrow steps and threw open the door to the attic. "We need to dust everything to get rid of spiderwebs," she said as Aggie and Lily followed her inside the room.

Aggie went over, lit the lamp, and then opened the shutters and windows. She looked around at the jumbled mess. "I be thinkin' dis place need be straightenin' up," Aggie fussed as she moved about. "How in tarnation can you find anything in all dis heah mess?" She shoved a box out of her path.

"You're right, Aggie," Ida May agreed. "This room just

needs a general overhaul and I know you are the one who can do it. I'll be glad to help."

"I want to help, too," Lily spoke up. "It was my things that caused all this mess. We were in such a hurry that everything was just thrown in here every whichaway."

Aggie straightened up, put her hands on her broad hips, and looked from Ida May to Lily. "Miz Ida May you gwine on back down dem stairs. Me and dis heah Miz Lily we kin do dis job jes' fine."

Ida May looked at Lily and smiled. "If you need me, just holler," she said. "I'll be in Janie Belle's sewing room."

Lily smiled and nodded back. She adjusted the scarf she had tied over her hair and tightened the strings on her big apron.

"And, Aggie, I'll keep an eye on the beans and ham you've got cooking for dinner," Ida May added as she turned to leave the room.

"Dat be fine. I be down in time to dish it all up," Aggie agreed as she moved about the room surveying the mess.

Ida May left and Lily waited to see what plans Aggie had next.

"Now, den I gits rags to clean wid and a bucket of water," Aggie said. "You jes' start straightening up things. I be right back."

Lily smiled at her and said, "Be careful on those narrow steps and don't get overbalanced with the bucket of water."

Aggie turned to look back as she walked across the room. "Miz Lily, I dun been cleanin' dis heah house since I wuz ten year old. I he'ped my ma and I ain't got hurt yit. I tell you 'bout dem old days when I comes back." She smiled and went on out the door.

Lily wanted to separate her things from Aunt Janie Belle's belongings. Her aunt's things had been added to over the years and were in no order at all. She began moving boxes that she knew belonged to her and stacking them in one spot. She noticed her things had not accumulated as much dust as the other stuff. But then, she had only moved in a few weeks ago.

Aggie returned with an armload of clean rags and a bucket of water with a mop stuck in it. She set it all down at the doorway and said, "Now, we needs to sweep a little as we goes 'fo we mops de flo'. I move de things so's you kin sweep, and den we shuffle dem all 'round and I'll mop. Den we dust everything off. Ain't no use dustin' 'fo we sweeps, 'cause dat makes mo' dust. Unnerstan'?" She looked at Lily with a big grin.

Lily smiled back. She understood that Aggie wanted to be in charge, which was fine with her. After all, Aggie worked for Aunt Janie Belle, and this was Aunt Janie Belle's house. "Sounds fine to me," she told the woman. "Now, where do we start?"

Aggie looked around and pointed. "Over dere by de window and we works our way toward de do'," she explained.

Lily followed the woman's instructions and soon realized that Aggie knew what she was doing. Everything was shaping up in some kind of order. The woman even knew which items belonged to Lily and helped her separate them from the other things. Lily's furniture was lined up on one side of the room with space enough to walk between pieces or open drawers when necessary. And her trunks and boxes were placed nearby.

All the time, Aggie kept up a more or less one-sided conversation.

"Yep, I bin heah since I wuz ten year old," Aggie explained as she worked. "My ma she come to work fo' Miz Janie Belle when Miz Janie Belle's pa built dis heah house fo' her and she married dat Mistuh Aaron. My ma she live heah till she die 'bout twenty year ago, 'cause Miz Janie

Belle she pay most money in de country heah. And Miz Janie Belle she git bossy sometime, but she got heart o' gold, she do. So I keeps workin' fo' her till one of us passes on. But you knows, I got me a man and married him and I cain't live heah no mo'. I got my own house t'uther side of town, so I jes' comes to work when Miz Janie Belle need me."

When the woman finally paused for breath, Lily quickly asked, "Aggie, you knew my mother, didn't you?"

"Corse I know yo' ma and yo' pa, too. Too bad whut happen to yo' pa. It jes' wudn't right. Dey's sumpin' wrong wid all dat," Aggie replied as she continued moving things around. "I knows, 'cause I seed dem two strange men down at yo' pa's shop, and they's all yellin' and ashoutin'—"

Lily quickly interrupted, practically shouting to make Aggie hear her. "You saw two strange men at my father's shop, Aggie?" she asked, her heartbeat quickening. "Do you know where they came from or what they were doing there?"

Aggie straightened up to look at Lily and slowly said, "I guess I dun put my foot in my mouth. My man Tinny he tole me not to git tangled up wid all dat trouble, 'cause dem men mought be dangerous and do sumpin' to us, so I better keeps my mouth shet." She bent over to continue moving things.

"But, Aggie," Lily said, quickly walking to her side and touching her arm. "Please help me if you know anything at all. I've lost my dear papa and I believe he was killed by some person, and not by a horse like they tell me. Please, Aggie, tell me what you know."

Aggie straightened up to look at her with a sad expression. "I'se sorry 'bout yo' pa but, Miz Lily, I'se skeered to talk 'bout it. 'Sides I don't really know nothin'." She continued working. "Now, let's git dis heah room cleaned up like Miz Ida May want."

Lily stayed by her side. "Aggie, don't you realize if someone killed my papa, that person is running around loose and might kill someone else? If you know anything, you need to tell me. Maybe it would help put them behind bars where they belong," she begged with tears in her blue eyes.

"Yeah, and dey jes' might come kill me if I gits tangled up wid dis," Aggie argued as she worked on.

Lily was so upset, she could hardly breathe. How could she find out if Aggie knew anything that would help her prove that her father had been murdered?

"Aggie, I promise I won't let anyone know you talked to me about it," Lily begged. "Whatever you tell me won't go any further."

Aggie mumbled as she lifted a box, "Den whut good it do you to know if'n you ain't plannin' on tellin' nobody? Let's git done heah so's I kin see to dinner."

Lily suddenly had an idea. If they didn't finish cleaning the attic that morning, Ida May would have Aggie come back tomorrow and finish. And if Aggie wouldn't discuss what she knew today, maybe Lily could think of some way to get her to talk tomorrow.

So she said to Aggie with a big smile, "Don't you think we ought to stop now and go on downstairs and finish up dinner? I know you want to get back home as soon as dinner is over with."

Aggie looked at her for a moment and then replied, "Well, we ain't finished yet up heah."

"But Aunt Ida May didn't say we had to get everything done in the attic this morning," Lily told her. "You could come back in the morning and we could finish then. I want to go through some of my things and will probably take a lot of stuff down to my room and Violet's room. But that will take a while, so why don't we just go on downstairs?" She watched Aggie set a box down and straighten up to look at her.

"Whatcha plannin' to do wid all dese things anyhow?" Aggie asked. "You got most a whole houseful up here."

"I'll put it in my own house when I move back in," Lily told her, wondering whether the woman knew what had really happened to her house.

"Humph!" Aggie said, glancing around the room. "Probably all be molded and rat-bitten by den. Mought as well sell it or give it away."

"Oh, no, no!" Lily exclaimed, excitedly running her hand down the top of the bureau from her mother's bedroom. "These things are my life. They could never be replaced."

Aggie put her hands on her hips and frowned as she said, "Now, Miz Lily, if you gwine give sumpin' 'way, why you wanta replace it?"

"But I don't want to give it away or sell it. I want to keep it all forever," Lily said sadly.

"What's in dem drawers and dem boxes and sech anyhow?" Aggie asked as she glanced up and down the room at Lily's belongings.

"Oh, Aggie, my mother's things and Papa's," Lily began. "Let's go down to the kitchen now and help Aunt Ida May get dinner ready." She started toward the door and looked back to see if Aggie would follow her.

Aggie scratched her head, blew out a big sigh, and said, "All right den. We comes back tomorrow early."

Then it was Lily who blew out a sigh, a sigh of relief. Her plan had worked.

Lily followed Aggie out the door. Aggie went on down

the hall on her way to the kitchen, and Lily stopped by the bathroom to clean up.

Ida May was just taking bread out of the oven when Lily came into the kitchen. Aggie had evidently cleaned up and was wearing a fresh apron as she dished up the beans from the big pot on the stove.

"What can I do to help?" Lily asked her aunt.

"Nothing in here, child," Ida May said. "If you could find your Aunt Janie Belle and Uncle Aaron and tell them dinner is practically on the table, that would be a big help. They're probably in the little parlor at the back."

Ida May was right. Aunt Janie Belle was doing some needlework, and Uncle Aaron was dozing in his chair with a book in his lap.

"You had a caller, dear," Aunt Janie Belle told her as she gathered up the material and placed it on a table next to her chair.

Lily looked at her in surprise and asked, "I did?"

"Yes, your friend Ossie came by to see if you'd like to go into town with him this afternoon," her aunt said as she rose. Uncle Aaron snapped awake and stood up. "Seems he's got the day off and has some reason to go. Said he'll be back by after he sees Roy about a few things."

"Well, do you have any idea as to when that will be? I mean, is he coming before we eat dinner? I'll have to dress if I'm going," Lily said as she glanced down at the blue gingham dress she was wearing.

Janie Belle started toward the hallway door with Uncle Aaron at her side. "No, no, I told him we're just about ready to sit down to the table and he would be welcome to join us, but he had promised to eat a bite with Roy while they talked business. So don't worry, you have plenty of time to eat and then dress, dear," her aunt assured her.

The three of them went on into the dining room, where

Ida May and Aggie had everything on the table and waiting.

"Everything smells good, Aggie," Janie Belle told her as Uncle Aaron helped her to be seated.

"Den thank Miz Ida May. She done most of it, and if it's all de same to you, Miz Janie Belle, I gwine eat while I cleans up de kitchen so's I kin hurry on home," Aggie said as she moved the bowl of beans closer, within Aunt Janie Belle's reach.

"That's fine, Aggie, and don't forget to take some of everything home with you for your supper," Janie Belle replied. She looked at Ida May and asked, "When do we need Aggie back?"

"Early tomorrow morning," Ida May replied as she passed the potatoes to Lily. "We're not quite finished in the attic and we might as well get that out of the way, and then Aggie could start on a general housecleaning before it gets so cold we have to have heat in all the rooms."

Aggie stood waiting. Janie Belle looked up at her and asked, "Would you be free to return tomorrow morning then, Aggie? I know you work for other people."

"I be heah bright and early and make breakfast 'fo we go up to dat attic, Miz Janie Belle," Aggie replied as she went through the doorway to the kitchen.

"Aunt Janie Belle, I appreciate your letting Aggie help me get my things in order up in the attic," Lily said as she picked up her fork.

"I'm glad to do anything I can for you, dear," her aunt replied. "You just take your time and get Aggie to do whatever needs to be done up there."

"Thank you," Lily said, smiling at her and then adding, "but right now I suppose I'd better hurry so I can get dressed before Ossie comes back."

"I'm sure he'll wait," Aunt Ida May said, smiling at her.

When the meal was over, Lily rushed to her room to change clothes. As she slipped out of the gingham and into a lightweight suit, she wondered why Ossie had asked her to go with him. She had not seen much of him since she had moved in with Aunt Janie Belle. He worked for Mr. Dutton in town and also ran a good-sized farm of his own, with Roy as his foreman. So Ossie didn't have a lot of free time, and she no longer lived right next to his house where he could step over for a few minutes now and then. She really missed him and would be glad to get a chance to talk with him.

Reaching into the pocket of the gingham, she took out the letters that she had been constantly carrying around with her.

"Maybe Ossie knows something about my father's business affairs," she said aloud to herself as she put the letters in the pocket of her skirt.

When Ossie arrived, Lily was glad to see him, but she could feel the slight tension that had crept between them ever since he had proposed to her. He had offered her a home for herself and her little sister, Violet, when she had lost her own home. But she couldn't marry him for that reason only, and she couldn't accept his proposal, because he was more like a big brother than a future husband. He was older and his young wife had died shortly after their marriage. Now at sixteen, Lily had never fallen in love and didn't feel ready to accept anyone's proposal.

"Come in," Lily said as she opened the kitchen door to his knock. The weather was getting chilly, and the kitchen was more or less the living room for the winter, except on occasions when guests came to visit. The wood fire in the iron cookstove was kept going all the time, and the long room stayed warm. One end held a cluster of chairs, a settee, stools, and the pedal sewing machine in the corner by the window.

"So you are going with me to town," Ossie remarked as he stepped inside and adjusted his spectacles. "Good idea to wear a warm suit. It's a little breezy out there."

Lily smiled at him and asked, "Would you like to sit down for a minute, or are you in a hurry to get on your way?" The two still stood inside the doorway.

"Since you are all ready to go, we might as well start out," Ossie replied. His serious brown eyes looked into her blue ones. "I have to stop at the office and then I have a couple of other errands in town. I thought we could have supper at the inn if it's agreeable with you."

"Oh, Ossie, of course, whatever you say, but I should run tell Aunt Ida May not to expect me for supper," Lily said, starting across the room toward the door to the hallway.

"You don't have to do that," Ossie called to her. "When I was by earlier, I told Miss Ida May we might be returning after suppertime." He smiled under his mustache. "She thought that was a good idea, that you should get out and do something besides staying home all the time."

"You and Aunt Ida May are in cahoots, I see," Lily said. "Well, let me get my hat and I'll be ready." She went to the sewing machine and took her hat from where it sat on the top of it and went to the mirror over the big sink to put it on.

Ossie had been holding his hat in his hands, and he opened the door for Lily and followed her outside. He put on his broad-brimmed hat and helped her step up into his buggy in the driveway.

"Thanks, Ossie," Lily said as she sat down and he came around the other side and got in beside her.

Neither one said anything for the first few minutes down the road, but then Ossie looked at her and said, "I'm sorry

I haven't been able to get over to see y'all very often since you moved in with your aunts, but today is the first day I've had off from the office since I returned from England. The cotton business is booming."

"I'm glad to hear that," Lily replied as she clasped her hands in her lap. She was so uncomfortable, she couldn't think of anything to say, but she tried to overcome it because she really loved Ossie as a brother. He had watched her grow up. He had been there when her mother had died. And he had tried to comfort her by proposing marriage when she was going through the sorrow of losing her father and her home.

"I spoke to Mr. Dutton again to remind him that you are still interested in finding work of some kind, and he said if anything at all turns up in the office he'll let you know," Ossie said as he drove along.

Lily quickly turned to look at him. "But, Ossie, didn't Roy tell you that I am setting up a sewing business at Aunt Janie Belle's, in the room that Aggie used to live in before she got married?"

Ossie glanced at her and replied, "Well, yes, he did, but I was thinking that may be slow getting started, and if something else came along in the meantime, you might be better off accepting other work, don't you think?"

Lily frowned and said, "Well, maybe, but my heart is set on the dressmaking business, and I believe I can make a go of it so that Violet and I can have our own home somewhere."

Ossie reached to squeeze her hand. "I'm sure you will turn out to be the best dressmaker in the countryside," he said. "And I'm also certain you will be able to move into a home of your own one of these days. If there is ever anything at all that I can do to help, just let me know." He reached to adjust his spectacles as he looked at her.

"Ossie, I have something I wanted to ask you about," Lily said as she pulled her mother's letter from her pocket and held up the envelope for him to see, then returned it to her pocket. "This is a letter I found in my father's desk that my mother wrote to him not long before she died. She said in it that she wanted me to have her jewelry, that it had been passed down for four generations in her family. Do you remember ever seeing my mother wear jewelry?"

Ossie frowned and thought for a moment. "No, I don't believe so," he said. "I was young when your parents got married and was running around about on my own business, but I do remember seeing your mother in what I thought were very expensive clothes, and she might have worn jewelry, too. I just don't know. Have you looked through everything?"

"I think I have, but Aggie and I are getting my things straightened up in the attic, and I plan on looking in every drawer, every box, every trunk, and everything else just to be sure," Lily said. "And then, Ossie, she said in this letter, too, that she had provided for Violet, and that my father was the only one who knew the details. Do you have any idea as to what she might have been talking about?"

Ossie adjusted his spectacles again, looked at her, and said, "Why, no, Lily, I'm sorry, but I couldn't imagine what she meant by that. Did you find her will—or your father probably had it probated when she died, I would think. But then, what about his will? Did you find it?"

Lily sighed deeply and said, "No, Ossie, I don't think my father ever had a will drawn up. He never mentioned one. And his papers are all in such a mess I will have a job getting things in order."

"A will is a pretty important piece of paper, Lily, so be sure you go over everything with a fine-toothed comb when you sort his papers," Ossie said. He turned to look at her and asked, "In fact do you know if he owned any other property besides your home place? If he did, that would solve a lot of your problems."

Lily anxiously looked at him and asked, "Do you think he might have, Ossie? I can't remember him ever mentioning any other property, can you?"

"I vaguely remember hearing him talk about some land along the Enoree River that he said he'd like to have. Seems like it had an old cornmill on it that had been abandoned," Ossie said thoughtfully.

"A cornmill? Maybe I could locate a cornmill over there somewhere and find out who owns it," Lily said hopefully.

"Yes, let's do that. I'll help you," Ossie promised. "I'll ask around in town and see if anyone knows anything about it. I don't know when I'd have time, but we could go to the courthouse in Greenville and check the records, too."

"Oh, thank you, Ossie," Lily said. "And I'll ask Logan about it. He might know something, or maybe Aunt Janie Belle and Aunt Ida May can help me. But you know, neither one of them has mentioned anything about my father owning other property, so I don't really have much hope."

"Your father kept his business pretty much to himself, Lily, so don't forget that. Other people didn't know everything about him and his dealings," Ossie reminded her.

Lily reached to pat Ossie's hand as she said, "Ossie, you have given me a glimmer of hope. As long as I can keep busy with any idea at all, I won't give up," she said. Tears filled her blue eyes. "I loved Papa so much. It's a shame things ended up in such a mess after he worked so hard all his life."

"I know," Ossie said, moving his hand so he could squeeze hers. "And always remember, it helps to talk about anything, anything at all. You see, just because of our conversation today you have several possibilities to look into.

Who knows? Something may come of what we've discussed."

Lily swallowed hard to control her emotions. "If I could only find out the truth about his death, I believe it would solve a lot of things. And I won't stop until I do find out exactly what happened to Papa, even if it takes me a lifetime," she told him as she straightened up in her seat.

"I don't believe the sheriff's conclusion that your father died from injuries caused by a horse, either" Ossie said. "Lily, anything you want my help on, just let me know." He pulled the buggy up in the shade across the street from Mr. Dutton's office and jumped down to throw the reins across the hitching post. "Are you coming in with me?"

Lily debated that question a moment and then said, "No, I'll just wait out here for you. I'll go walk up and down the street for exercise." She caught up her long skirts, and Ossie reached to help her down.

"I won't be long," Ossie promised. "If you get tired of walking or I get unexpectedly delayed, come on inside."

"I will," Lily promised as she started down the sidewalk, and Ossie went to the door of the building where Mr. Dutton had his cotton business.

As she strolled along, Lily thought about their conversation. Ossie did give her some new ideas to explore. And she was itching to go on with all of it. Patience had never been one of her virtues, and now she was wishing the time away until she could get back home and question her aunts. They might know something they had never even thought of mentioning to her. It might take her a long time, but she would not stop as long as there was the slightest hope.

She also needed to get started on her sewing business, and that would have to cut into some of the time she needed to look for information about her father's business.

She suddenly realized her footsteps felt light and optimistic for the first time since she and Violet had returned from England.

At the inn that night with Ossie, she ate one of the few good meals she had had since coming home. The mountain of obstacles before her somehow didn't look quite so high after her conversation with Ossie.

When she came home from town, she found that Logan had hung the curtains in her new sewing room. Everything was in place, and she was ready to begin her battle for independence.

Chapter Five
The Past in the Attic

The next morning, Lily and Aggie returned to work in the attic. Lily had tried and tried to think of some way to get Aggie to talk about the two strange men she had seen with Lily's father in his blacksmith shop, but she had not come up with anything. They had been working for almost two hours.

"I'd like to take some of these things down to my room, Aggie," Lily said as she bent to look at the contents of several boxes. "I can go through all this down there and bring back what I don't need right now."

"You jes' show me whicha ones, and I he'p, Miz Lily," Aggie replied as she came across the room.

Lily pointed to two boxes and said, "These right here. If you would carry one for me, I can tote the other one." She stooped and picked up one of the boxes.

"I sho' can," Aggie replied as she lifted the other one.

They took them down to Lily's bedroom and set them in a corner.

"Is dey mo' you wants to bring down?" Aggie asked. "Den I bettuh git dinner cookin'."

"Oh, no, thank you, Aggie," Lily said. Then she thought of a possible way to get Aggie to talk. "You and Aunt Ida May and Aunt Janie Belle had been baking bread that morning my father died, hadn't you? And Aunt Ida May went to take two loaves to my father. Aggie, what time did you pass the road to the blacksmith shop and see those strange men talking to Papa?"

Aggie frowned as she looked at Lily and then, taking a deep breath, she said, "I guess it ain't gwine to hurt nuthin' if I tells you dat. I wuz on my way to work heah dat mornin' early, 'cause I cooked breakfast when I got here."

"Did your husband bring you to work? How did you get here?" Lily asked.

"No, Tinny, he go to work t'uther direction. I brought de cart cause he work close 'nuff to walk."

"What did those men look like? Did you not know them?" Lily quickly asked before Aggie would have time to think about her response.

Aggie shook her head and said, "No, Miz Lily, ain't never seed dem befo'. Dey dressed up, not like whut our men wear 'round heah."

"So they must not have been from around here," Lily decided. "Have you seen them since then?"

Aggie quickly walked toward the door as she said, "Miz Lily, I ain't s'posed to talk 'bout dem men, you knows dat. Now I go cook up some dinner." She hurried out the door.

Lily sighed as she watched her go. "Maybe I can find out more later," she said to herself. She looked at the boxes and added, "I'll get started on this."

She sat on a low stool and began removing the contents of one box and laying the stuff on the floor. The things from her bedroom bookshelf in her own house had been haphazardly packed in the boxes. After she had it all out on the floor, she decided to leave it there and go back up to the attic to search for her mother's jewelry while no one was around.

She started with the first piece of furniture belonging to her, thoroughly searched the drawers, and continued down the line. The contents of her mother's bedroom set had not been disturbed since she had died, and now Lily carefully examined all of it and placed it back. Tears came into her eyes as the belongings brought back memories. She was familiar with most of the personal articles because she had taken care of her mother for several years before she died. Finding no jewelry at all, Lily moved on to her father's things. She almost broke down when she found his pipe and tobacco stuck in a dresser drawer. She took out the pipe and held it tight in her hand. It was the same pipe Violet had taken possession of when they first came home from England and learned of his death.

"Papa! Papa!" Lily cried as she felt the loss from that day all over again. She remembered the shock she had felt when she learned that her father was already dead and buried before she and Violet had arrived home. If only her father had not insisted that she and her little sister go to live with their mother's sister in England while he tried to pay off debts, he might still be alive today.

Lily slipped the pipe into her apron pocket and continued searching the drawers. Suddenly her hand hit something hard and cold underneath some loose papers in the bureau. She used both hands and pushed the papers aside. Underneath were his keys, the keys she had finally found in his blacksmith shop before she had to move out of her house.

"Probably a key to everything," she said to herself as she

flipped through the bunch, the key to the house, one to his desk, and—

"Lily, are you up there?" Aunt Ida May called from downstairs, interrupting her thoughts.

Lily added the keys to her apron pocket, causing it to sag from the weight as she hurried to the doorway.

"I'm here, Aunt Ida May," she called back.

"There's someone to see you," her aunt replied from the landing below.

Lily looked over the rail and asked, "Someone to see me? Who is it?"

"Come on down where we can talk a minute, dear," Ida May said.

Lily thought Aunt Ida May was acting awfully strange about it. Who could the caller be? She glanced down at her apron and touched the scarf tied around her head as she descended the steps.

"Who is it?" she anxiously asked as she got to the landing where her aunt was waiting.

"I didn't know what to say when he asked for you, so I just said wait right here and I'll see if she can come to the door. He's waiting on the front porch," Ida May hurriedly said.

Lily frowned and asked, "He who, Aunt Ida May? Who is it?"

"It's that young man, Wilbur Whitaker—" she began to explain.

Lily interrupted angrily, "What does he want with me? How dare he come here? Where is he?" She clenched her fists. She had met Wilbur Whitaker on the ship coming home. He had seemed to be interested in her, but she had not been sure about him.

"He's on the front porch, dear, but don't—" Ida May answered.

Lily rushed past her and practically ran downstairs to the front door, jerked it open, and confronted Wilbur Whitaker, who was learning against a post. When he saw her, he straightened up and smiled.

"What do you want? Don't you dare come onto this property!" Lily yelled at him as she stepped out onto the porch. "Go home where you belong."

"Wait a minute! I haven't done anything to you!" Wilbur managed to say.

"Your father took my house away from me, and I don't want anything to do with his son. Now, get off this property!" Lily shouted.

"That's not so. My father didn't take your house away from you. He paid for it legally when the tax people sold it," Wilbur said as he stepped closer, towering above her by a least a foot. His brown eyes flashed with anger.

"It was not legal, and someday I'll prove it if it's the last thing I ever do," Lily said, her voice trembling with rage.

"Lily, let's don't stand here and argue. I came to see you—" he said.

She interrupted, "I don't care why you came here. Just get off this property!" She stomped her foot.

Ida May had followed Lily to the door, and now she stepped outside and told Wilbur, "You have been requested to leave. Do I have to get someone to show you off this property?"

Wilbur frowned, blew out his breath, and started to walk down the steps. "You'll be sorry. Remember that," he said as he went to his horse, which was tied by the driveway.

Lily watched until he mounted and rode away. He didn't even look back. She sighed with relief and turned to go back inside the house. Ida May followed her into the hallway.

"I'm sorry, Lily," Ida May said. "I just didn't know what

to say to him when he knocked on the door and asked to see you."

"Never mind, Aunt Ida May," Lily said, feeling exhausted from the confrontation. "But if he ever comes back, I'd appreciate it if you could just make him leave. I don't want to ever see him again."

"I'll remember that, dear," Ida May said. "Now, why don't you get cleaned up a little. I believe dinner is almost ready."

"I'll be right back down," Lily promised as she hurried up the stairs and Ida May went down the hallway toward the kitchen. Why had Wilbur suddenly shown up? She decided she wouldn't even think about him.

Once in her room, Lily found herself to be trembling and had trouble removing her dirty apron and headscarf. She threw them into a corner of her room and went to the bathroom to wash up. She didn't even check her dress to see if she had soiled it or not. Glancing in the mirror and not really seeing anything, she pushed back her hair and went back downstairs.

Aunt Janie Belle and Uncle Aaron were not in the parlor, and Lily went on into the kitchen and saw they weren't there either. Ida May was helping Aggie dish up the food.

"Where is everybody else?" Lily asked.

"I checked on them on my way down. They're in your Uncle Aaron's office working on papers and said they'd be here shortly," Ida May explained.

Lily went to the cupboard to get dishes and turned back to ask, "Are we eating in here or in the dining room?"

"In the dining room, dear," Ida May said. "We've got the fire going in the fireplace in there and it's warm enough."

So Lily took the dishes into the dining room and set the table. She wondered why Aunt Janie Belle insisted on eating in there when there was a table big enough for at least ten people in the kitchen, which was much more cozy.

Lily's visitor was not mentioned at the dinner table, so evidently Aunt Janie Belle and Uncle Aaron had not seen or heard Wilbur. And as soon as the meal was over, Lily went back to her room, put on a fresh apron, and tied another scarf around her hair. She glanced at the dirty ones she had thrown in the corner before dinner, and she realized pretty soon she'd have all her aprons and scarves dirty and would have to do some washing. She should be finished that afternoon with searching all her belongings in the attic for any jewelry her mother had owned. She had looked in all the drawers and boxes. The only things left were the trunks, and there were several of them. Quite a few were old, and Lily did not remember ever having looked inside them.

When she got to attic, she continued her search. Bending to read the faded shipping label on an old trunk, she read aloud, "London, England! My mother must have brought this one from England with her!"

She tried the lid and found it unlocked. The metal around the edge was stuck, but after using various things in the attic to pry at it, she finally opened it. The smell of lavender met her nose as she looked inside. Filling the trunk's tray were odds and ends that evidently her mother had wanted to keep, such as a pressed rose—now almost disintegrated—several ribbons, hairpins, a shoe horn, lace-edged handkerchiefs, an ivory fan, and a small beaded bag. Lily immediately grabbed the bag and opened it, but there was only a neatly folded handkerchief inside.

"Oh, well, let's see what's under here," she mumbled to herself as she tugged at the tray. When she lifted it out, she was surprised to find the most beautiful, lacy, expensive-looking dresses she had ever seen. She lifted them out one at a time, shook out the wrinkles, and walked to a floor mirror standing in the corner to hold them up in front of her. Her mother must have been approximately her size when she was young, because each one seemed to be an exact fit as she held them against her.

"Mother! Her English clothes she must have brought with her!" she exclaimed. Sadly returning them to the trunk, she added, "She must have packed them away when she became so ill."

Lily found shoes, cloaks, hats, and other apparel in the other old trunks. She decided her mother had had an expensive collection of clothes.

"And if she had expensive clothes like this, she probably had some real jewelry to go with them," Lily said to herself as she looked around the room. Then she suddenly realized something else. "If Mother had all this, and probably jewelry, too, she must have had lots of money or her family must have been well off."

Lily thought about her visit with Violet to their mother's sister, Aunt Emma, in England last summer. Lily had not thought her aunt was wealthy. She had a nice home and a servant and evidently had inherited an income—inherited an income? Lily thought about that again. If Aunt Emma had inherited money, then it had to have been from relatives, since Aunt Emma had never married. And since her mother was Aunt Emma's sister, was there a possibility she could have inherited money, too? How could she find out? Aunt Ida May and Aunt Janie Belle didn't seem to know much, and neither did Logan when Lily had asked about jewels.

Suddenly she remembered something. *The friends Mother came with from England when she met my father! These friends had come to visit relatives here in the United States. Who were they? I'll just start asking questions and somehow, somewhere, I'll find out.*

Lily had never really discussed relatives with her mother and didn't know much about that side of her family, except for Aunt Emma. And as she thought about it, Aunt Emma had said all the family had passed away except for her. Could there possibly be another relative, maybe a distant relative, who had known her mother? Aunt Emma certainly wouldn't discuss her mother's past when Lily had asked questions while there except to say Lily's grandparents had both died years ago.

"Now that I think of it, Aunt Emma always changed the subject when I mentioned relatives, and during the short time Violet and I were there we didn't meet very many friends of Aunt Emma's," Lily talked to herself as she sat on the top of her mother's old trunk. "And Mama was so sick for so many years we just didn't talk about such things. Oh, how I wish I had."

Lily was brought back to the present by her little sister, Violet, calling her as she came up the steps. Violet's white puppy ran ahead of her and pounced across the room to greet Lily by licking her ankles.

Lily bent and shook her long skirt at the animal. "I'm in here, Violet. Please come and get this puppy. Aggie and I have just finished cleaning this place and we don't want any accidents from the puppy to mess it up."

"I'll take him down to the yard. I just wanted to let you know I'm home from school," Violet told her, looking up with her blue eyes.

Lily remembered a promise she had made to Violet, and she said, "Why don't you just take the puppy down to the yard and come back up here? I want to show you something."

Violet's eyes widened in anticipation as she said, "I'll be right back. Wait for me." She ran for the door.

"Be careful on the steps. I'll wait. You don't have to run," Lily said as she followed the child to the doorway.

Violet was back shortly, eager to see what Lily had in mind. She followed Lily across the room to their mother's old trunk.

"You see this trunk here?" Lily asked, pointing to the shipping label on it. "That says it came from England, so it must have been the trunk our mother brought with her when she came to the United States and married our father. Now I want to show you what's in it."

Violet watched closely as Lily lifted the lid and removed the tray, revealing the fancy dresses beneath. She took out the blue one that lay on top and held it up.

"Oh, Lily, can I wear that dress? It's beautiful!" Violet said, reaching to touch the smooth material and lacy trim.

"I don't think it would fit," Lily said, holding it up against her. "You see, it's more my size. But all these belonged to our mother, Violet. She must have brought them all from England."

"But, Lily, when I get big as you, can I wear it, please?" Violet begged as she softly touched the ruffle around the neckline.

"All right, when you get big enough, if you still want to wear it you may," Lily promised. "And look at all these other dresses." She lifted several others out of the trunk. "And there's a trunk over there with fancy shoes, bags, and lots of other beautiful things."

"Can I see, Lily? Please!" Violet said, excitedly jumping up and down.

"All right but we have to be careful because everything is old and we might damage things if we get in too big of a hurry," Lily reminded Violet as the child rushed to look through the dresses.

Lily took her time and showed everything that had belonged to their mother to her little sister. She had not seen Violet so happy since before they had learned of their father's death. She made a silent decision that she would copy the blue dress for Violet. The style was not outdated and not too grown-up for the child. That would be her present to her little sister for Christmas. It would be a tie for Violet to their mother, and she didn't want the child to ever forget her.

And she also thought she'd write to Aunt Emma and describe the dresses in the trunk to see if she knew whether they came from England or not.

"Couldn't we just hang these dresses up where we could see them all the time?" Violet asked as she went back to the trunk.

"They would get dirty and faded," Lily explained. "Let's just leave them in the trunk for the time being. Then when you are big enough, we'll come back up here and you can try them all on."

Violet straightened up and looked at her sister seriously as she said, "I'll eat lots more so I'll grow tall enough."

"I think you'd better go downstairs now and go outside to play with the puppy," Lily said as she began closing the other drawers and things. "Where is your kitten?"

"He's outside, too, but he won't let me pick him up if I'm holding the puppy, so I could only bring the puppy up here," Violet explained.

"Now, Violet, you've got to come up with a name for that puppy, and the kitten needs one, too," Lily told her. "We can't just keep on calling them the puppy and the kitten. You have a name. They need names, too."

"Don't worry about it, Lily," Violet said as she ran

across the attic to the door. "I'll decide on names for both of them one day soon."

Lily laughed as she heard the child hurrying down the stairs.

The trunk containing the dresses was the last one she needed to close. Lily bent to smell the lavender and then picked up the tray to place it back inside. As she lifted the tray, she bumped the edge of the trunk slightly with one corner, causing the contents to shuffle around. She stopped to straighten out the things in the tray and noticed the ivory fan didn't seem to lie flat. She picked it up to be sure it was closed tightly, and as she started to put it back in the tray, she noticed a lump in the silky lining.

"What's wrong? Did I damage something?" she asked herself as she laid the fan aside and reached to smooth the lining. She felt the lump beneath and noticed there was a slight rip in the material. "Goodness, did I tear it?"

She pulled at the rip and realized there was something under it. She excitedly stuck her forefinger inside the small opening and felt something hard. Without even thinking about what damage she might be doing, she pulled the thread in the seam of the lining and jerked back the material.

"Oh!" Lily exclaimed as she stared at an old tintype hidden in the lining. She pulled it slowly out. As she stared at the small, framed photograph, she was amazed that her mother had evidently hidden the picture.

Rushing over to the window in the fading light, she studied the man and woman in the photograph. Her heart beat wildly as she gasped, "My grandparents! They've got to be! My mother's father and mother! My mother looked just like the woman when she got sick and older looking."

Lily squeezed the tintype, and tears sprang into her eyes. "But why would my mother hide a picture of her parents?

Why didn't she keep it out somewhere so she could look at it?

"Oh, Mama, I don't know why, but I do know this is going on my bureau right next to the one I have of you and Papa," Lily declared.

She laid the picture aside, returned the tray to the trunk, and closed the lid. Rushing over to the windows, she closed sash and shutters, picked up the tintype, and hurried down to her room. When she placed the old photograph next to the one of her mother, she could see the strong resemblance. Of course, it had to be her grandparents.

But why had her mother kept it hidden? Oh, the many mysteries confronting her! It would take a long time, but she would solve them all.

Chapter Six
Logan's Idea

While she was helping Aunt Ida May prepare supper that night, Lily thought about the tintype. She decided not to mention it to anyone. No one here had ever seen her grandparents, so they wouldn't know whether it was them in the picture or not. And she didn't want Violet thinking it might be of their mother's parents if it really wasn't.

Logan came in the back door while Lily was setting the table. According to Aunt Ida May, supper would be in the kitchen tonight and not the dining room, as requested by Aunt Janie Belle.

"Are you all finished?" Ida May asked the man as he stepped inside with his wide-brimmed hat in his hands.

"I sure am, Miss Ida May, and I jes' wanted to say I'm done, so I'll be gettin' on home now," Logan told her. He turned toward the table and said, "Howdy, Miss Lily."

"I'm glad to see you, Logan, but you know my name is just plain Lily, please," Lily said with a smile. "Else I'm going to have to call you Mr. Logan."

Logan smiled and said, "Yes, ma'am, I jes' keep forgettin' I don't work for you no more." Turning back to Ida May, he said, "I'll drop by in the morning to see if you need anything else."

"Wait, Logan," Ida May said as he put his hand out to open the back door. "Janie Belle says to ask you to stay for supper since you were nice enough to take the horse to get it shoed. She knows you're about the only one who can handle that animal out on the highway."

Lily listened with surprise. Aunt Janie Belle had extended an invitation to Logan to stay for supper.

Logan hesitated before he replied, "You don't have to feed me for doing that. I was glad to be of help."

"Logan, I am giving you orders to get washed up now. Supper is practically on the table," Ida May said. She was standing at the stove. As she put a lid back down on one of the pots she turned to look at him.

"Yes, ma'am, yes, ma'am, I won't turn down a meal cooked by you, Miss Ida May," Logan said as he quickly hung his hat on a peg by the back door and walked over to the sink.

"That's a clean towel I hung up there for you," Ida May told him as she pointed toward the sink. "Now, get a move on."

Logan looked at Lily and grinned when Ida May went back to the stove. Lily grinned back as she set six places at the table. He hurriedly cleaned up at the big sink and dried with the clean towel.

Lily was glad Logan was staying, because she wanted to ask some questions of him and of her aunts, and this way she would have them all together.

Violet came in the back door as Aunt Janie Belle and Uncle Aaron came into the kitchen from the hallway. Lily was relieved to see that the child did not have either of her pets with her.

"Wash up, Violet," she told the child. "We're about ready to eat."

Violet ran to the sink and stepped up on a stool to reach the water as she called to Logan, who was standing nearby, "Logan, you're going to eat with us!"

Before the man could respond, Janie Belle hobbled toward the table and said, "Hurry up, child. We're sitting down. Logan, please be seated over there." She indicated a chair next to Violet's where Lily normally sat.

Lily went around to the other side and took the place next to Ida May as everyone sat down. She wondered why Aunt Janie Belle had put Logan in her place.

After Uncle Aaron returned thanks for the food, Violet held her plate out to Lily. She said, "I want lots of everything so I'll grow big enough to wear my mother's dress. Remember, Lily?"

Lily took the plate and noticed everyone's eyes looking instantly at the child.

"Your mother's dress?" Aunt Janie Belle questioned.

"Oh, yes, my mother's dress. Lily found lots and lots of them in a trunk in the attic and let me see them," Violet replied, smiling at the lady. "They're old dresses."

Then Lily felt everyone turning to look at her as she spooned beans onto Violet's plate.

"You found dresses of your mother's?" Aunt Janie Belle asked Lily. "In a trunk?"

"Yes, ma'am," Lily answered as she added a biscuit to Violet's plate. "I didn't know about them. I suppose they were stuck away in our attic at home and I never noticed the trunk. It has a shipping label showing it came from England."

"Indeed!" Aunt Janie Belle said.

"I believe they are clothes she brought with her when she came to the United States," Lily explained. "If you and Aunt Ida May looked at them, maybe you might remember seeing her wear some of them. They're all expensive-looking and fancy."

"Your mother had some nice-looking clothes when she first came here," Ida May said.

"But then she tried to look countrified, to fit in with the people around here I suppose, and she stopped ever wearing the expensive clothes," Aunt Janie Belle said.

Lily looked at Logan and asked, "Do you remember seeing her wear fancy, frilly, lacy dresses made out of expensive-looking material? You were working for my father then and you were around there more than anyone else."

"Yessum, I believe I do remember such clothes," Logan replied as he set down his coffee cup. "I can still hear her tell your pa to get dressed up so she wouldn't look so out of place."

"Oh, she did?" Lily said in surprise, because she remembered her mother wearing gingham and calico before she became disabled and was finally bedridden. "I can remember my mother back to when I was probably four or five years old, but I don't remember seeing the clothes I'm talking about."

"Child, you would have been too young to be present when your parents had socials or dressed to go to someone else's," Ida May reminded Lily.

"I suppose so," Lily agreed. She looked around the table and asked, "Does anybody know who the friends were that my mother came with to the United States and who they went to visit in this country?"

The adults looked at each other as if deciding who would answer.

Uncle Aaron finally spoke, "Your papa, Charlie, met

your mother in Charleston. He had gone down there on some business, and if I remember correctly, your mother was staying at the home of the man your father went to see. The people were relatives of your mother's friends."

Lily gasped in surprise. All these years she had never heard about this. Yet everyone in this room seemed to know. She had failed to ask questions of her parents that she should have asked years ago.

"Do you remember who it was my father went to see? The man's name?" Lily asked excitedly as she laid down her fork.

"Sorry, I'm getting old and forgetful," Uncle Aaron said, shaking his head.

"I did know, but I can't think of it right now," Janie Belle said.

"And I don't believe I ever heard it," Aunt Ida May told her.

Lily looked at Logan, who had not said a word. She could tell he was uncomfortable at the table with Janie Belle and Aaron.

"Logan, did Papa tell you anything about who he was going to see?" Lily asked.

"Your grandpa was still around at that time and I worked mostly with him," Logan said. "Your pa tended to business for him. And you know something strange? Your mother came up here alone and they were married in your family's church. I always wondered why her friends didn't come for the wedding."

"Oh, I know that much," Aunt Janie Belle told him. "Her friends didn't come up here with her because they had gone back to England."

"I know they were married in our church. Papa always told me that much," Lily said. "And it's written in our family Bible also."

Lily had another idea. "Logan, do you suppose there would be any record in Papa's papers as to whom Grandpa Tad was doing business with in Charleston?" she asked.

"Maybe, but it would be like looking for a needle in a haystack," Logan replied.

"But if there's anything on paper about it, the papers should still be in Charlie's business things, because it's not that long ago. Lily is sixteen and the two were married the year before she was born, May the third, I believe," Aunt Ida May said.

Lily looked at her and smiled. "You just don't realize what a ton of papers my father had," she said. "And nothing is in any kind of order."

"That's a shame, but then your father worked so hard night and day, he just didn't have time to do everything," Aunt Janie Belle said.

"Yes, I know," Lily said sadly. "I wish I could have helped."

"Child, you had your hands full running the house, waiting on your mother, and raising your little sister," Aunt Ida May reminded her.

"As soon as I get started on my sewing, I'll have to take time to try to put his business papers in some kind of order," Lily replied. "And, Logan, go ahead and bring whatever you have to mend or make, and I'll get it done for you."

"I'll drop it off one day soon," Logan told her.

"More," Violet demanded as she held up her empty plate.

"More of what?" Lily asked as she took it.

"Potatoes and biscuits and gravy," Violet told her as she watched.

Lily put the requested food on the plate and handed it back to Violet. She wondered if her little sister had been listening to the conversation about their mother, and tried to remember what all had been said. Violet would be asking questions later if she had been paying any attention.

"Maybe your Aunt Emma would know something about these friends of your mother's," Aunt Janie Belle suggested as she finished her cup of coffee.

"I'm going to write to her," Lily replied. "About that and about the dresses I found in the trunk. But it takes so long for mail to cross the ocean, there's no telling when I might hear back from her."

"In the meantime, if I can remember that name, I'll let you know," Aunt Janie Belle said as she pushed back her chair.

Everyone rose from the table.

"I thank you for the good food, but I must needs be goin' now," Logan told Aunt Janie Belle. "I'll drop by to-morrow to see if you need anything."

"And I thank you, Logan, for taking the horse for us. There's not a man on our place here that can control that horse on the highway," Aunt Janie Belle replied.

"Yes, and if we can ever do anything for you, just let us know," Uncle Aaron added.

"Lily, you go write your letter to your Aunt Emma. Ida May and I will clean up the supper dishes," Aunt Janie Belle said.

"No, no," Lily protested. "You and Uncle Aaron go sit and rest somewhere. I know how much trouble you have with your feet. And I like keeping busy."

"Yes, Janie Belle, go sit somewhere and get off your feet. Lily and I work pretty well together, and it won't take long to get done," Ida May added.

"Well, if y'all insist," Aunt Janie Belle replied. Turning to her husband, she said, "Let's just sit in the parlor and read a while before bedtime."

Logan walked over to get his hat from the peg as Aunt Janie Belle and Uncle Aaron left the room. Violet waited to get scraps for her pets.

"Logan, I want to talk to you a minute if you have time," Lily said.

"Of course I do," Logan said as he held his hat in his hands.

Lily looked at Aunt Ida May across the room and said, "If you don't mind, I'll let Violet's puppy and kitten in to eat while I talk to Logan outside." She made a motion behind Violet's back that let Ida May know she didn't want Violet to hear whatever she was planning to discuss with Logan.

Ida May understood. "That's fine, dear," she replied. "Violet and I will soon have supper ready for her animals." She smiled down at Violet, who was holding a plate.

When they stepped out onto the back porch, Lily felt the chill of the night air and realized it would soon be cold weather. She rubbed the sleeves of her dress and followed Logan to the hitching post where his horse was tied.

"There's something I wanted to tell you in strictest confidence," Lily began. "I have promised I wouldn't tell anyone, but I have to discuss it with you. It might help us solve something."

"Of course," Logan said, looking down at her. "It won't go no further. You can rest assured about that."

"Aggie and I have been cleaning the attic, and she slipped up and told me something her husband had forbidden her to talk about," Lily began. "On the day my father died she came to work here early; she said it was before breakfast. She was alone. When she passed the road to Papa's blacksmith shop, she said she saw two strange men down there with Papa and they were all yelling and shouting at each other."

"You don't say!" Logan said with a low whistle.

"She said that they were strangers, that she had never seen them before, and that they were dressed like city folks," Lily continued. "What do you make of that?"

"You say her husband forbade her to talk about it. Why would he do that?" Logan asked.

"She said he was afraid the men might be dangerous and might do something to them," Lily explained.

"Then he must have been suspicious of the men, or else he must know something," Logan reasoned as he scratched his head.

"But, Logan, don't forget," Lily reminded him. "Aggie and her husband are Negroes, and it would be their word against the white people's if they told anything they know. You know how that is sometimes."

"I know, and it's a pity," Logan replied. "But if they really know something, we might could prove whatever it is with their help. Do you think you could get them to talk about it?"

"No, Aggie said she wouldn't tell me anything else because I would go and tell somebody and they'd be in trouble," Lily explained.

"These two men could be connected with whatever happened to your pa," Logan said. "I know your Aunt Ida May found him up in the morning sometime before dinner, and he—" he paused and looked down into Lily's blue eyes in the moonlit darkness. "Your pa had already—been gone awhile by then."

Lily's breath caught in her throat as she thought about her father. She couldn't answer, and Logan continued.

"See if you can get Aggie to talk anymore," Logan said. "I just remembered one angle that might help convince her to tell you anything else she knows. Remind her that your grandpa rescued her mother out of poverty and the slums when her father died. He was the one who hired Aggie's mother to work for your Aunt Janie Belle."

Lily was surprised to hear that, but she knew her grandfather was known far and wide for his good deeds. "How did that come about?" she asked.

"Aggie's father worked for your grandpa for several years, but they had a falling out over something and her pa quit. He went out drinking, got in a fight, and got himself killed," Logan explained.

"Does Aggie know all this?" Lily asked.

"I suppose so. She was old enough to see and hear what was going on," Logan said.

"She told me she and her mother came to live at Aunt Janie Belle's when she was ten years old because Aunt Janie Belle paid the highest wages in the community," Lily said.

"That's right," Logan said. "But that was your grandpa paying that, and he had an agreement with Miss Janie Belle not to let it be known."

Lily thought about what Logan had told her for a moment, and then she asked, "Do you think it's right to bring this up and make Aggie feel like she owes me a favor?"

"It's all accordin' to how you put it," Logan said. "Just let her know that you know all this I've just told you. Then one day later bring up the fact that no one is willin' to help you find out what happened to your pa. But knowing Aggie, you might not have to wait. She might just start talkin'."

"Well," Lily said, hesitating. "I'll tone it all down a little and let her know in bits and pieces."

"If she does talk anymore, get in touch with me," Logan said. "I'm usually workin' over at my place and not hard to find."

Lily stepped back as he mounted his horse. "Don't

worry," she said, "I'll let you know anything at all that she says. Good night."

"Night now," Logan said as he rode off up the driveway.

Lily hurried back inside the house to help Aunt Ida May in the kitchen. Violet was sitting on the floor playing with the puppy and kitten.

"You need to go to your room now, Violet, and get calmed down before bedtime," Lily told her.

Violet rose, picked up the puppy, and tried to get the kitten, but it hid under the stove. She started for the door as she glanced at Lily.

Lily decided to ignore the fact that the child was carrying the puppy to her room. She began drying the dishes Aunt Ida May had washed and said, "I'll come and tuck you in, in a little while."

Violet still didn't say anything, but left the room with the puppy in her arms.

"What am I going to do about these animals?" Lily asked her aunt. "If Aunt Janie Belle finds out Violet is taking them to her room, she'll throw us out."

"Don't worry about it, child," Ida May said. "Janie Belle is having such a time with her feet lately, she doesn't pay any attention to anything else."

"I'm sorry about that, but you know, Aunt Ida May, she can really make a big fuss if she gets upset," Lily said, stacking the dried dishes on the shelf by the sink.

"Right now she's trying to remember the name of that man in Charleston that your papa went to see," Ida May told her. "She gets her mind on one thing and won't rest until she gets it solved."

"I sure wish she could remember who he was," Lily said. "Of course that's a long time ago, and the man might be dead, or moved, or left town, or something by now. And even if I had the name, I might never be able to track him down."

"And again he might be right where he was seventeen years ago," Ida May reminded her as she hung up the dish-rag and Lily spread out the drying cloth beside it.

"You know Ossie goes to Charleston a lot on business for Mr. Dutton, and if I had the name, I could ask him to look for the man," Lily said.

"You're right," Aunt Ida May replied. "Maybe Janie Belle will remember the name." She walked over to the back door and locked it. "Right now I think we both need to get some rest. You go ahead and see about Violet, and I will finish closing up down here. Your Aunt Janie Belle stuck her head in the door while you were out talking to Logan and said they were going on upstairs for the night."

"Good night, Aunt Ida May," Lily said, putting her arm around the woman's shoulders and giving her a squeeze.

"Good night, child, you sleep well," Ida May replied as she returned the hug.

Lily went upstairs and found Violet already asleep, but at least this time she had put on her nightclothes and was under the covers. The puppy was curled up beside her, and Lily quietly lifted him and put him in the box in the corner. He didn't protest. Just as she went out the door, she saw the white kitten run in from the hallway and disappear under Violet's bed. She knew where that animal would end up for the night—right beside Violet.

In her own room Lily put on her nightclothes between trips to her bureau to gaze at the tintype she had found in her mother's trunk. She finally decided to turn the picture on its face so it wouldn't be visible for Violet to ask ques-tions about. If she could ever prove that it was a picture of their grandparents, then she would show it to her little sister.

She thought about the search of the attic. As far as she could tell, she had examined everything up there that belonged to her, and there was no sign of any kind of jewelry. She was so disappointed that she couldn't figure out what to do next.

Walking over to the corner, she picked up the dirty apron and scarf she had thrown there earlier and suddenly remembered the letters in the apron pocket. She put her hand inside and pulled them out. Then she felt her father's pipe and keys in the other pocket and extracted them. Carefully laying his pipe on her bureau, she jingled the keys in her hand and came up with a wild scheme.

She held the key to her own house here in her hand. When the house was sold, the extra key had been given to the tax people. Suppose something was accidentally left in her house, something that might contain jewelry? Dare she go look?

She knew the visit would upset her emotionally. But, on the other hand, she might discover something that might prove valuable. Of course she could still only call it *something*, because she had no idea what to look for.

Thinking further, she realized she would have to go in the daytime so she wouldn't catch anyone's attention with a light. She would also have to walk, because if she rode Lightnin', she would have to tie him up and someone might see him.

She crawled beneath her covers, stuck the keys under her pillow, and tried to think the whole scheme through. It was such an exciting idea she almost never went to sleep that night. But she finally decided to go look for that *something* —unless she changed her mind in the morning.

Chapter Seven
Rain and Mud

L ily's fitful sleep was disturbed by the sound of heavy rain. Later she heard her clock in the hallway strike four in the morning. Aunt Janie Belle had allowed her to place the big clock in the corner near her bedroom door.

"If it's still raining hard after breakfast, I'll have to take Violet to school in Aunt Janie Belle's buggy," she groaned to herself as she turned over to face the window, against which the wind was blowing the rain.

Then she had another thought and raised herself up on her elbow. "That would be a good excuse to go out. I could leave the buggy somewhere and walk over to our house and search the place," she said to herself. She decided she was definitely going to hunt for anything that might have been left behind when they moved from the house in such a hurry.

She lay down and tried to go back to sleep, but she tossed and turned. Finally, as the clock was striking five, she dozed. It seemed only moments later that she came awake again and realized something had hit her bed. She rose up to look around in the darkness and was greeted by a squeaky "meow" as Violet's kitten walked across her covers.

"I just don't know what I'm going to do about you," Lily told the kitten as it curled up on the crumpled quilt near her feet.

Lily stretched and yawned a few minutes and finally decided to get up and look at the clock to see what time it was.

Quickly lighting the lamp on the table by her bed, she carried it out into the hallway. Looking up at the big face on the clock, she said to herself, "Six-thirty! I might as well get dressed. Aunt Ida May is probably already in the kitchen."

Back in her room, she hastily put on a dark calico dress as she looked out the window. The rain was still coming down in sheets, pelting the glass.

The kitten was asleep on her bed, and Lily reached to pick it up. "Come on," she paused, remembering the kitten had no name. "You've got to have a name. In the meantime, I'm going to call you Little Bit because you're just a little bit of a kitten." The kitten purred as she held it in her arms. "We're going down to the kitchen where it's warm," she added as she carried the tiny animal downstairs with her.

Lily set the kitten down as soon as she stepped inside the kitchen, and it ran for the warmth of the cookstove where Ida May was already at work.

"Good morning," Ida May greeted her.

"Good morning, Aunt Ida May," Lily replied as she went to the sink to wash her hands. "That little animal found its way into my bed last night. I hope it doesn't visit Aunt Janie Belle's room some night."

"Don't worry about it," Ida May said. "Your Aunt Janie Belle has always kept the door to her room closed at night." She smiled and said, "But now I leave my door open just a crack."

Lily looked at her and smiled. "I suppose I'm going to have to be sure Violet closes her door to the hallway if she insists on taking the animals to her room at night." She went to the cupboard and took down plates and began setting the table.

"And speaking of Violet, I'm afraid you're going to have to take her to school. It's raining so hard she'll be drenched if she walks, and it's right cold out there in all that wet." She set the percolator on the stove to make the coffee.

"I know. I had already thought about that," Lily replied as she glanced out the window. It was dark outside, but she could see the rain blowing against the glass.

Aunt Janie Belle and Uncle Aaron didn't come down for breakfast. So after Lily, Violet, and Ida May finished eating, Lily took Violet to school.

Lily pulled up to the school as close as she could in the buggy and told Violet, "Now, if it's still raining like this, I'll be here waiting for you when you get out this afternoon."

"Bye," Violet replied as she jumped down from the buggy and ran toward the door of the log schoolhouse.

Lily was glad to see that her little sister was interested in school. She shook the reins and drove back down the road as she tried to decide where she could leave the buggy so that no one would see it while she walked on to her father's house. Then she remembered there was an old abandoned house on the other side of the road, and a stable still stood behind it. It wouldn't be a great distance to cut across onto her father's land and get to the house from the back side.

Rain was standing in deep puddles in the driveway to the

old stable, and Lily had to practically creep along in the buggy to keep from sliding. When she arrived at the stable, she was able to drive straight into the building through the open entrance. Once inside, she found the dirt floor was mostly dry because the roof seemed to be in good shape. But she sighed in disappointment as she looked forward and saw the dense growth that blocked the other end. She would have to back the buggy out when she left. This was Aunt Janie Belle's horse, and Lily wasn't sure how he would behave.

"Oh, well, I'll manage somehow," she said to herself as she looped the reins around a shaky old post inside the stable. "I'll worry about that when I come back. Right now I've got to get going."

Lily pulled the hood on her cloak over her hair and felt in the pocket for the key to her father's house. Then lifting her long skirts, she hurried back down the abandoned driveway, sidestepping the puddles when possible. Pausing at the road long enough to look up and down to be sure no one was in sight, she crossed it and ran into the muddy field that had been her father's property. Circling behind trees here and there, she finally came to the rear of the house. The key in her pocket was the one to the back door.

Pausing in the heavy rain behind some shrubbery bushes, she looked around the yard. No one was in sight.

Her heartbeat quickened with emotion as she raced for the back door, slipped the key in, turned the lock, and pushed the door open. She paused on the threshold to get control of herself. Pains like daggers pierced her heart as she glanced around the kitchen, now empty of all signs that she had once lived there.

"Papa!" she whispered to herself as she pushed the door shut and locked it, putting the key back in her pocket. "I can still feel your presence here."

Her eyes clouded over with tears. She pushed back the wet hood and pulled a handkerchief out of her skirt pocket. Wiping her face, she said, "Tears won't do any good. I've got to be sensible about this." Her voice trembled as she took a deep breath.

She looked down at her feet and saw that the cloak was dripping water onto the floor. Removing it, she hung it on a peg by the door and shook out the hems of her long skirts where they had got wet.

"I suppose I'll begin here in the kitchen, although it's unlikely anything of value would have been kept in here," she said to herself. She began opening doors and drawers in the huge built-in cabinet. Nothing there. She searched every inch of the large pantry. Not even a grain of meal in there.

Moving on, she opened the door to a closet in the hallway. The day was dark, and it was impossible to see inside. She slowly ran her hands around the shelves and walls.

Lily kept searching and finally covered the entire downstairs of the house without even finding a piece of trash left behind. Sitting down on the bottom step of the front stairs to the second floor, she tried to brace herself for the visit up there where everything was so much more personal and full of memories. She would have to enter bedrooms, now empty, and her father's office without its furnishings.

"I've got to move on and finish this," she said aloud to herself. She stood up and began to slowly ascend the stairs.

Upon reaching the upstairs hallway, she was relieved to see dim light streaming in. Evidently the shutters were not closed on the bedroom windows. She would be able to see what she was doing up here.

Going into her mother's bedroom first, Lily searched every inch of the room and found only a single tortoise-shell hairpin lying on the floor in a corner. Stooping, she picked it up and ran her fingers over the smooth surface.

"Mother!" she said with a catch in her breath. "Somehow we lost this when we moved." She squeezed it tight and then slipped it into the pocket of her full skirt.

As Lily moved back out into the hallway, she heard a metallic click downstairs, then a squeak as the back door opened, and loud voices entered the kitchen below.

Lily's heart beat so hard, she was afraid someone would hear it. She was trapped upstairs! And she was sure one of the men downstairs was Mr. Whitaker.

"This is a good place to meet to get out of the rain while we make our plans," Mr. Whitaker was saying.

The other man spoke in a lower tone, and Lily couldn't quite understand what his reply was or who the voice belonged to. It did not sound familiar. She held her breath, worried that they would come up the steps, and she had no place to hide.

"I brought something to write on here," Mr. Whitaker continued, "but it would be more comfortable if we had something to sit on."

The other man murmured a reply that Lily could not understand.

"I know where we can sit. Seems like one of the bedrooms upstairs has a large windowseat. Let's go see if we can find it," Mr. Whitaker replied.

Lily felt her whole body pulse with fear. What would she do? They were coming upstairs!

"My bedroom window!" she whispered to herself as she raced for it and closed the hall door behind her. Running across the empty bedroom, she went to one of the windows facing the front and tugged at it.

"Come on! Open!" she demanded as she threw all her strength into raising the window sash. It came up so suddenly, she almost fell outside. She lifted her long skirts, stepped out onto the roof of the front porch, and pulled the window back down. Crouching in the rain, she looked for a way down. "The trellis at the end of the porch!" she cried, then she hastily waddled over to it in a stooped position.

The trellis should bear her weight without any trouble, she decided. But there was a rosebush growing on it. Without taking time to worry about that, she lifted her skirts, tucked them into the band of her skirt, and lay down on her stomach to wiggle onto the trellis.

"Whew!" she cried to herself as she felt the thorns on the rosebush. But that didn't slow her up. She gritted her teeth and worked her way down to the ground, landing in the evergreen shrubbery, which had sticky points on its leaves. Quickly extricating her skirts from the bushes, she leaned against the house to catch her breath and to try to figure out how she could get back to the old stable and her horse and buggy without being seen by the two men inside the house.

"The windowseat," she repeated to herself. "There's a windowseat in my mother's bedroom, which is on the front of the house, and there's a windowseat in my father's office, which is on the corner with windows looking out toward the front and side. Which one would the men go to?"

All of a sudden Lily began to violently tremble. Her teeth chattered and her legs wobbled. She knew she had to get back to the horse and buggy immediately. She managed to creep around to the back of the house, staying close to it, and then she stepped out into the bushes in the backyard. Without looking back, she hurried through the soggy field as fast as she could with her heavy, wet clothes. She finally made it to the road.

"Thank the Lord," she said, out of breath as she approached the drainage ditch that she had to cross to get onto the road. When she had gone over it to the house, she had been able to jump across. Now it was deep with water from the rain. She realized her wet clothes hindered her jumping it this time. Slowly edging down toward the water, she figured she could make it across if she narrowed the distance.

Then without warning, her feet slid out from under her in the mud, and she grasped in the air to regain her balance. Failing that, she fell flat on her face across the ditch. She screamed and tried to scramble to her feet in the slippery mess.

At that moment she heard a horse coming down the road. It slowed and the rider stopped to ask, "May I be of help?"

Lily glanced up as she finally made it to a squatting position on her feet. Wilbur Whitaker was looking down at her from the horse. She couldn't speak.

"My, my, Miss Lily Masterson!" Wilbur exclaimed when he saw her face. He jumped down from his horse and said, "Let me help you." He reached out a hand to her where she still squatted on the bank of the ditch, trying to wipe the mud from her face with her wet skirt.

"No, no, no! Go away!" she screamed at him as she managed to get to her feet, still in slippery mud.

"Look, you need a hand to get out of there," Wilbur insisted, still extending his hand. "Come on."

"Get away from me, Wilbur Whitaker!" she yelled at him. She was starting to tremble from the cold.

"What on earth are you doing in that ditch anyhow?" Wilbur asked as he stood there. "Where are you going out here in the rain with no coat?"

"None of your business! Go away!" she insisted.

Wilbur grabbed at her and managed to catch her hand. He pulled her up the bank against her will, with Lily fighting all the way. Then suddenly she swayed and almost fainted. She shook her head and took deep breaths, but she was freezing and felt the strength draining from her whole body.

"Come on, Lily," Wilbur told her as he looked closely at her. "I'll take you home."

Wilbur tried to pick her up to place her on his horse, but she mustered every ounce of remaining strength and fought with him. At that moment a cart came down the road. Lily heard it and looked to see who it was. As it rapidly came closer, she was relieved to see that it was none other than Logan.

Logan stopped his cart and jumped down. "What's going on here?" he demanded as he stepped up to Lily and looked at her muddy clothes. "Miss Lily, are you all right?"

"I was just trying to help her," Wilbur explained. "She had fallen in the drainage ditch here."

"Logan, p-p-please t-t-take m-m-me h-h-home," Lily said, shivering so much she could hardly talk.

Logan reached to help her and Lily said, "I can make it on my own. I h-h-haven't b-b-broken anything." She walked toward his cart.

Logan helped her step up into the cart while Wilbur watched.

"I'm sorry you wouldn't let me help you, Lily," Wilbur said as he mounted his horse. "I hope you are going to be all right." He turned and rode off in the opposite direction.

Logan quickly pulled a blanket out of a box under the seat and placed it over Lily's head and around her shoulders. He jumped into the cart and raced down the road to Janie Belle's house without asking another question. Lily was too cold to try to talk anyway.

Pulling up in the driveway at the back, Logan jumped down and hurried to the door to knock. Aunt Ida May answered it. Logan went back, picked up Lily in his arms, and brought her into the kitchen. Ida May was shocked to see Lily in such a condition.

"What happened?" her aunt asked as she pushed a chair over next to the warm cookstove. The old man put Lily in the chair and began rubbing her hands as Ida May quickly brought warm water and a washcloth to bathe her face and hands. Luckily she only had a few pricks from the rosebush on the trellis.

"Do you need help getting her up to her room?" Logan asked.

Lily heard that and said, "No, I'm going to stay right here. Logan, please don't go. I need to talk to you." She shivered again.

Ida May quickly spoke up, "Logan, you just stay here with her while I go up to her room and bring down some dry clothes." She hurried out of the room.

"Logan, I'm in trouble," Lily said, shaking from head to foot.

"I'd say it looks that way," Logan replied. He pulled up a cane-bottom chair next to her. "Miss Lily, where in tarnation you been out in that rain with no coat?"

"I went to my house," Lily began.

"Without a coat?" Logan questioned. "And what you been doin' at your papa's house?"

Lily suddenly remembered the buggy. "Oh, Logan, I forgot," she said. "I left Aunt Janie Belle's horse and buggy in the old stable by that deserted house across from ours."

"I'll get it, no problem," Logan said. "But you got problems here. Don't you know you could get awfully sick from all this gallivantin' 'round?" His tone of voice was severe, and he showed worry in his old face.

"That's not all," Lily continued. But as she heard Aunt

Ida May coming back down the hallway, she said, "Please don't tell Aunt Ida May."

Her aunt came in the room with clothes thrown over her arm. She hurried to Lily and laid the things down on a chair nearby. Looking up at Logan, she said, "I reckon you need to step into the hallway or somewhere so I can get some dry, warm clothes on this child."

Logan nodded and said, looking at Lily, "Yes, ma'am, Miss Ida May. But I got an errand to run right now, so I'll go do it, and I'll be back in a little while."

Lily looked up at him and said, "Thanks, Logan, but please do come back soon as you can."

Logan winked at her as he replied, "Will do." He went out the back door.

Ida May brought more warm water and helped Lily bathe and change into dry clothes. She didn't ask questions. All she was interested in was whether Lily was hurt or not. She wrapped a blanket around Lily after they finished and put her feet up on a stool by the stove. Then she brushed out Lily's long and blonde hair, which had lost most of its pins.

"Now, all we need is hot tea," Ida May told her. She went to the cabinet and said, "And I'll just make up some hot tea, stronglike, with a glob of honey in it. That ought to help straighten you out."

Lily leaned back and closed her eyes as her aunt hurriedly made the drink. She was really in a predicament. Her cloak was hanging in the kitchen back in her father's house, and the key to the house was in the pocket. If someone found it before she could retrieve it, she wasn't sure what the consequences might be.

"Now, I want you to drink every drop of this, just as hot as you can bear it," Ida May said, pulling over a small table by Lily's chair and placing the cup of hot tea on it.

Lily opened her eyes and looked at her aunt. "I'm sorry to be so much trouble, Aunt Ida May," she said as she lifted the cup. After taking a small sip, she blew on the hot concoction. It felt like it had blistered her tongue.

"It's got to be red hot to do any good, Lily," Aunt Ida May told her as she sat down, watching. "And you're no trouble to me at all. I love you like a daughter and want to help you all I possibly can in anything that comes along, no questions asked." She looked into Lily's blue eyes.

"Aunt Ida May, I'll explain as soon as I get to feeling better," Lily promised as she continued taking sips from the cup of hot liquid. In between sips, she piled her hair back up on her head now that it was dry.

Lily realized her aunt was wondering how she had got in such shape, where her cloak was, and where Logan had found her. But she was just too worried and too tired to explain right now. And she wasn't sure she wanted her aunt to know she had gone back to her father's house.

She certainly didn't want her aunt to know she would have to go back to her father's house again to get the cloak and the key. And she couldn't figure out how she would do that because the door would be locked. How would she get inside? Oh, what a mess she had got into!

Logan returned in a little while, and as Ida May rose to begin dinner, he whispered to Lily, "It's back and in the barn."

"Thanks, Logan," Lily whispered to him.

Ida May was busy at the stove and she looked back at Logan and said, "Now, you're staying for dinner, no question about it. So just take off that coat and sit down."

Logan hesitated, but Lily said, "Please stay."

"All right, Miss Ida May, but I'll have to make it fast after I eat," he said. "Got a couple more errands and then

I'll jes' stop by and pick up little Miss Violet from school so she won't end up getting all wet."

Lily had forgotten about that. She smiled up at the man as he hung his coat and hat on pegs by the back door and came to stand beside her.

"Thanks, Logan, I really appreciate that," Lily said. "I hate to think about going back out in that rain."

"No, no, you're not going back out in that rain," Ida May told her from the stove, "even if I have to go get Violet myself."

"No, ma'am, you don't need to go out and get all wet. I said I'd get the little tyke from school," the old man insisted.

Lily straightened up in her chair and began removing the blanket from her shoulders. "What can I do to help prepare dinner, Aunt Ida May?" she asked.

Ida May walked across the room and put a hand on Lily's shoulder to keep her from rising. "Not one thing but just sit in that chair and get warm," she said. "Now, don't get up."

"In that case, Miss Ida May, I think I would know how to set the table if you want," Logan offered with a big smile.

Ida May looked at him and grinned as she said, "That's the best offer I've had from a man in a long time. You know where the dishes and silverware are over there in the cabinet. And just set three places for us. Janie Belle and Aaron are having trouble with their joints today in this wet weather, and they're staying in their rooms. I'll take them a tray later."

Logan went over to open the cabinet. He looked inside and glanced back at Aunt Ida May. "We be needin' glasses or cups, Miss Ida May?"

"Logan, you know you can't drink coffee out of a glass, and you know we always have the pot on the stove," Ida

May replied with a big smile as she stirred a pot on the stove.

"Yes, ma'am, Miss Ida May, you're right," Logan answered with a big grin. "You're a lady that's always right, 'bout most things anyway."

As Lily listened to the banter between her aunt and Logan, a strange idea came to her. Logan and Aunt Ida May always seemed to get along so well together. And as she watched them closely, she wondered if either one of them had thought about that, or if either of them was in love with the other one.

As she continued thinking, she knew Logan was a lot older than her aunt, but he didn't act old. And she knew Logan was poor and didn't have much education. Her aunt had been to the best of schools and must still have an income of her own. Lily knew that when her grandfather, who was Ida May's father, died, his estate had been equally distributed among his children—her father, her Aunt Janie Belle, and her Aunt Ida May.

"Are you up in the clouds there, or are you sick, Lily?" Ida May was asking her as she came back to the present. Her aunt was looking at her.

"Oh, I was just thinking," Lily said. She sat up straight in her chair. "About a lot of things," she added.

"It's about on the table, child," Ida May told her as she walked past the little table holding Lily's tea. "And you haven't finished your tea."

Lily looked at the cup and picked it up. "I'll bring it to the table with me," she said. She rose and dropped the blanket onto the chair. She was feeling better now that she had got warm. She walked over, set the cup at her place on the table, and turned to ask, "Could I help you bring the food to the table or something? I've been really lazy."

"No need for you to do that with me helpin' your aunt,"

Logan said. He walked over to the stove and asked Ida May, "Want me to take something over to the table for you?"

"Why, sure enough," Ida May said as she pulled the hot biscuits out of the oven and dumped them onto a platter. "Here. Take these."

Logan took the bread to the table as Lily watched and listened. Then she suddenly remembered Wilbur Whitaker showing up when she fell into the ditch, and her mind began trying to figure out where he had come from. His father had been in the house, and then Wilbur turned up on the road outside. Could they have been together in the house? She had not been able to figure out who the other man was because he didn't talk loud enough for her to hear him or for her to understand what he was saying. She wasn't able to even try to identify the voice of the other man.

But then Mr. Whitaker had said something about that being a good place to meet. He wouldn't say that to his son, would he? As far as she knew, Wilbur lived at home, or at least that was the impression he had given her when she had met him on the ship coming home from England that summer.

And now she would have to watch for a chance to talk to Logan. She needed to let him in on her secret.

Chapter Eight
Possible Solutions

L ily sat around worrying about her cloak and the key all afternoon. When Logan brought Violet home from school, Aunt Ida May was working on some needlework in Aunt Janie Belle's sewing room, and Lily sent Violet upstairs to play in her room. The child insisted on taking the little animals with her, and Lily didn't object. This was her chance to discuss things with Logan, who had agreed to stay for a cup of coffee, since the pot was already on the stove.

"Logan, I haven't told Aunt Ida May what happened this morning. I know she's wondering, but I wanted to talk to you about things first," Lily began. She and Logan sat drinking coffee at the end of the kitchen table.

"Well, I'd say you'd better stay away from your papa's house," Logan told her. "Don't belong to you anymore."

"I know, Logan, but there was a special reason I went over there," Lily began explaining. "You see, I was hoping I'd find my mother's jewelry had somehow been left behind when we moved."

Logan looked at her in surprise. "Your mother's jewelry? Miss Lily, you don't even know for sure she had any jewelry, and how could it have been forgotten when you moved out?"

"I'm sure she had some jewelry, but I just don't know where to look for it," Lily replied with a frown. "I don't think my father would have got rid of it under any circumstances because the letter says it is for me. Remember?"

"I know that, but if you can't find any, then I'd say there's not any," Logan told her. "Don't get your heart set on something that's just not real."

"I believe my mother had a special place to keep the jewelry, and it must have been a place that was safe and secure," Lily said as she put down her coffee cup. "Because she said in her letter that my father would know where to find anything of value. To me that means a secret hiding place somewhere, where no one else would be likely to find the things. And since I've been through everything we own in the attic, I've decided the hiding place must be in the house. Therefore the jewelry would have been overlooked when we moved."

Logan thought about what she said for a moment, and then shaking his head, he said, "You sure make it sound like that's what happened, but I'd say you'll be in deep trouble if that Whitaker man catches you in that house."

"That's what I wanted to tell you," Lily said. "I was in the house this morning. I have a key that I found in my father's belongings. It fits the back door. I walked over there from the old stable and let myself in."

"Without a coat?" Logan asked. "In all that pouring down rain?"

"No, I had on a cloak with a hood, but it was so wet when I got inside the house, I took it off and hung it on the peg at the back door while I looked around," Lily explained. "And while I was upstairs I heard Mr. Whitaker and another man come in the back door. I couldn't hear the other man well enough to figure out who he was." She paused as she thought about that.

"And did Whitaker see you?" Logan asked as he sipped his coffee.

"Oh, goodness, no!" Lily exclaimed. "I ran into my bedroom and went out the window onto the roof of the front porch."

"Miss Lily!" Logan said in surprise.

Lily smiled at him and said, "And I managed to crawl down the rose trellis and get back to the road. But I had to leave my cloak behind. That's when I fell in the muddy ditch where you found me."

"Then what was Whitaker's son doing there?" Logan asked.

"I don't know. He just happened to come along when I fell. I have no idea where he'd been or where he came from," Lily said. "I've wondered about that. Maybe he was the other man with Mr. Whitaker in the house, but Mr. Whitaker said something about the house being a good meeting place, and I don't think he'd talk like that to his son because, as far as I know, Wilbur lives at home with his family."

"Do you reckon he knew you had been in the house?" Logan asked.

Lily felt a tingle of fear as she thought about that. "I don't know," she said. "But I sure hope not."

"So now you've got to get your cloak out of the house, is that right?" Logan asked.

"Yes, because it has the door key in one of the pockets, and I don't want to lose that," Lily said. "And that makes it practically impossible for me to get back inside to get the cloak because now I don't have a key to unlock the door."

"Hmmm!" Logan said thoughtfully. "Is it possible to go back through the window you came out?"

"I don't know how I'd get up on the roof to get to it," Lily said.

"And that rose trellis is not all that strong. I'm surprised it held your weight when you came down it," Logan told her.

"If I knew there was a window unlocked on the first floor, I could try getting through it. Even though the windows are high off the ground, I could get something to step on to reach one," Lily said. "But I can't go climbing up to each window to see if it's unlocked. That would take too long and someone might come by."

"I could probably reach the windows well enough to see if any of them are unlocked," Logan said. "But, mind you, I didn't say I would. That Whitaker man is dangerous to deal with. I hear tell he's already shot at trespassers on the property where he lives."

Lily's heart flipped at that. The man really was dangerous. And if he had caught her in the house, there's no telling what he might have done.

"Let me warm our coffee," she said, rising to bring the pot from the stove as she thought about Mr. Whitaker and the danger of carrying out her plans to search the house.

"That's enough, thank you," Logan held his hand toward his cup as Lily absentmindedly continued filling it all the way to the brim.

Lily realized what she was doing and said, "I'm sorry." She refilled her cup and returned the pot to the stove.

As she sat back down, she looked at Logan and asked, "Please think real hard. Can you remember ever hearing of a hiding place for valuables in our house? Maybe when Grandpa Tad was living? He would have known every crack and corner in it."

Logan thought for a moment and shook his head. "Can't say I do," he said. "I do know your grandpa sometimes hinted that all his valuables were not in one place, and to me that would indicate a special drawer, closet, bin, or something where he would have put important stuff."

"As I grew up I never heard of anything like that, but then I was not the nosy kind of child who examined everything and asked questions about everything," Lily said. "Much to my sorrow now, I can see where I should have asked about a lot of things that it's too late to ask about now."

Logan looked at her and said, "I might be able to check out one window at a time on the first floor and then keep watching for a chance to check out another and another until we know whether one is unlocked or not. But mind you, this would take some time."

"Oh, Logan, could you?" Lily asked, and then she realized he might get caught. She sighed and said, "On the other hand, I'm not sure I want you to do it and run the risk of Mr. Whitaker finding out about it."

"Well, it's like this," Logan told her. "I'm sure Whitaker knows that Ossie has Roy keeping the yard clean around the house, and I could just volunteer to help, without telling Roy the reason, of course."

Lily thought about that. "You think you could try the windows without Roy knowing?"

"I'm sure I could. While he's working in the front, I could work in the back and keep moving around to a different place from where he is," Logan assured her.

"Then if you find a window unlocked, are you going to let me know so I can go through it and get my cloak and key?" Lily asked.

"No, ma'am, not a chance," Logan quickly replied. "I'll go in and get it myself."

"Logan, I don't want you to take chances for me," Lily protested.

"I can get through those windows much easier than you can, Miss Lily," Logan told her. "And I'll have an excuse to be in the yard in the first place. But you know it's awfully rainy and muddy out there, and we'll have to wait for things to dry out a little bit before we can go rakin' leaves over there."

Lily thought about that for a moment and she had to agree. There was no other solution to her problem. Logan could do this much easier and faster than she could.

Logan promised to let Lily know if he found a window unlocked and was able to get inside. However, that would not be today, Lily realized.

"Be sure to bring your sewing next time you come by, because I need to get started on this sewing business if I'm ever going to," Lily told him.

"Will do, soon as I remember," Logan told her as he left.

Lily went to her room and spent the rest of the afternoon composing a long letter to Aunt Emma.

She started, "I am writing to inquire if you knew who the friends were that my mother came to the United States with and who the relatives were here that the friends took my mother to see."

She didn't give her aunt the reason for asking questions, but said she would like to look the people up.

She continued writing, "And I found a whole trunkful of fancy, expensive dresses that evidently belonged to my mother. Do you know anything about these? Did she bring these from England? I'm sketching a small picture of two or three on an extra sheet of paper, which I'll enclose with this letter, and I hope you can identify them."

Then Lily thought a long time about the jewelry mentioned in her mother's letter before she finally decided to ask Aunt Emma about it.

"I have been through all my mother's belongings and have not found a single piece of jewelry, so I'm wondering if she had given it all away or sold it before she died," Lily continued. "Aunt Janie Belle and Aunt Ida May vaguely remember seeing her wear a pearl necklace at a social years ago, and a strand of the pearls broke. They said my mother was really anxious to find every single pearl that had fallen to the floor. Therefore, they thought they must have been real."

Lily glanced at the tintype on her dresser and went to stand it up to look into the faces of the man and woman in it. She gazed at it for a long time and finally decided not to mention this photograph to Aunt Emma. She would do that later. Right now Lily had a lot of questions she needed answers to from the lady, and she didn't want to bog her aunt down with too much at one time.

"I don't believe the tintype could be as important as the other things I need to know anyway," she said aloud to herself as she laid the photograph flat on its face again. "I'll ask about this later."

And she didn't mention her mother's letter to Aunt Emma. The letter was too dear to her heart to talk about it easily with others.

Ossie came over that night after supper to visit for a little while. Aunt Janie Belle and Uncle Aaron had stayed in their rooms all day, and Lily had taken their supper up to them. Ida May was back in Janie Belle's sewing room, working on her needlework. Violet was playing around the cookstove with the puppy and the white kitten.

"Come in," Lily said when she answered Ossie's knock and opened the back door. "How did you know we have chocolate cake in the safe?" She laughed.

Ossie hung his hat and coat on the pegs by the back door and smiled as he replied, "I can always count on chocolate cake in this house, with plenty of coffee."

Violet came running to join them and started begging, "Chocolate cake? I want some!"

"All right, wash your hands, and I'll give you a small piece because it's just about bedtime for you," Lily told her little sister. Violet raced for the sink.

Lily went to the pie safe, took out the huge chocolate cake Ida May had baked that day, and carried it to the table. Ossie was right behind her with cups and plates from the cabinet. Violet managed to dry her hands in time to get the silverware out of the drawer.

When they were settled down at the long table, Ossie asked, "Well now, Violet, what have you named your puppy and your kitten?"

Violet sighed, frowned, and looked up at him as she devoured the chocolate cake. "Nothing yet," she said. "I just can't think of names for them yet, but I will." She rolled her blue eyes as she crammed her mouth full. "Mmamamam! This is so good!"

Lily smiled at her and said, "Now, Violet, you just have to come up with names for the little animals. I have started calling the kitten 'Little Bit,' and if you don't hurry up and name it, that's going to be its name."

"No, no, no!" Violet said, gulping down the glass of milk with her cake. "That won't do at all! He won't always be a little bit of a kitty. Someday he's going to grow up real big, like that!" She measured the air with her hands.

"All right then, until you do name him, that's what I'm going to call him," Lily said.

"I know lots of names better than that," Violet said as she finished her cake and milk.

"Now that you're finished, I think you'd better go up to

your room. You don't have to get in bed right now. You have your books to read, and I'll come up in a little while and tuck you in," Lily told her.

Violet sighed and slipped down from her chair. Looking in Lily's direction, she snatched up the puppy and ran from the room.

"One day Aunt Janie Belle is going to catch up with her for taking the animals to her room, but I hate to forbid it," Lily said to Ossie. "The pets seem to fill a place that would be empty, since our papa is not here anymore. I don't know what I'd do to keep her happy without them."

"I wouldn't worry about your Aunt Janie Belle," Ossie replied as he drank his coffee. "I think she would understand if she stopped to think about it. I know she's huffy-puffy sometimes, but she really has a heart of gold."

"I know, but I don't like doing things in someone else's house that I think might irritate the person," Lily said.

"I really came over to see if you're all right," Ossie said, changing the subject and looking closely at Lily.

"All right?" Lily questioned as her heart thumped. Did he know what she had been up to today?

"Yes, Roy was just coming out onto the road in the cart to go when he looked down the road in the opposite direction and saw Logan pick you up and put you in his cart. And Roy said that Whitaker fellow, the young one, was there, also. What happened?"

"Oh!" Lily exclaimed, trying to decide what to tell him. "I slipped into the ditch, and the mud was so slippery I couldn't get out."

"What were you doing out on the road in the rain without a coat and hat on, if I may ask? Now, I'm not meddling. I'm just trying to look after you and be sure nothing happens to hurt you," Ossie explained as he pushed his spectacles up on his nose. His brown eyes were full of concern.

Lily felt herself turn hot and red all over with embarrassment for some reason. She didn't know what else to do but repeat the story she had told Logan.

"So you see, everything backfired on me today," Lily ended.

Ossie was plainly shocked. "Lily, that Whitaker man is known to be dangerous. Why, he even shot at trespassers on his property—"

"I know," Lily interrupted. "Logan told me about that. But, like I said, I believe my mother's jewelry must still be in that house, and I won't stop until I find out one way or another."

"I'm not sure what Mr. Whitaker would do to you if he caught you trespassing on that land," Ossie said. "After all, he does own it now. And I would advise you not to go near the place again."

"But I have to get my cloak and the key out of there somehow," Lily said. She had decided not to tell him Logan's plan to get them. She didn't want the old man involved.

"Promise me you won't do anything right away," Ossie said. "I'll help you somehow, but I have to go to Charleston tomorrow for Mr. Dutton and don't know how long I'll be gone. Please wait until I come back before you do anything else."

"But, Ossie, every minute that cloak and key are in there, there's a greater chance Mr. Whitaker will find them," Lily said.

"If he does, maybe he'll think they were left there when you moved out," Ossie suggested.

"But that's not the important point. I want that key back so I can go inside the house and finish searching for my mother's jewelry," Lily argued.

"A few days won't matter that much," Ossie said. "Roy

says he has only seen Whitaker over there two or three times since you moved out. In fact, Roy saw him leave from there today right after he saw you get into Logan's cart."

Lily gasped and asked, "Did he see me?"

"No, Roy said he went in the other direction, and he doesn't believe Whitaker even looked down the road toward you," Ossie said.

Lily breathed a deep sigh of relief.

"Well, since he didn't see me this time, he won't be watching for me to come back," Lily said.

"Look, why don't you wait until I at least get back from Charleston before you go nosing around there anymore?" Ossie asked.

"I'm sorry, but I can't promise, Ossie," Lily replied as she ran her forefinger around the rim of her coffee cup.

"All right then, I'll check with you when I return to see what has transpired while I was gone," Ossie said.

Suddenly Lily realized Ossie was going to Charleston—the city where her mother had had friends and where her father had met her mother.

"Oh, Ossie, I know a few things about my parents that I didn't know before," Lily began. "Aunt Janie Belle and Aunt Ida May told me that my father went to Charleston on business for his father, and that he met my mother at the home of the man he went to see. Nobody remembers the man's name, but I've just written and asked Aunt Emma if she knew who he was, because he was a relative of the friends that my mother came with from England."

"Goodness gracious!" Ossie said. "Please take a breath." He laughed. "That gets to be a complicated situation, doesn't it?"

"If I only knew the man's name, I would ask you to see if you could find him," Lily told him.

"Yes, I would have to have a name and I'd be glad to do it for you, but what brought all this curiosity on?" he asked.

"I just realized that I know very little about my mother, and I should have been asking questions as I grew up," Lily said sadly. "I would like to get to know that family in Charleston if I could track them down."

"I understand," Ossie said, reaching to pat her hand. "And as soon as you do find out the man's name just let me know, and I'll make it necessary to go back to Charleston. As you know, Mr. Dutton has lots of business dealings down there, and I'm usually the one who goes to see about them."

"Oh, thank you, Ossie," Lily said, looking into his brown eyes. "I always appreciate everything you do for me and Violet, and for always being there to talk to."

"I hope someday it will be more than talk," Ossie said with a big smile as he adjusted his spectacles on his nose.

Lily smiled back and dropped her gaze. She had turned down Ossie's proposal of marriage because she loved him only as a good friend. She seriously doubted she would ever love him in the way he wanted, but she knew he would go right on hoping.

Chapter Nine
Sewing Begins

The next morning, Lily was delighted to be awakened by the birds chirping outside in the darkness. And not a sound of rain could be heard. She remembered it was Friday, the day for Aggie to come clean house. Maybe she would get a chance to talk with the woman as Logan had suggested.

She hurriedly dressed and went down to the kitchen. Aggie was already there, busy at the stove. Ida May was setting the table in the kitchen.

"Well, y'all are up and at it awfully early, aren't you, or did I oversleep?" Lily asked, smiling at the two women.

"No, you didn't oversleep," Aunt Ida May said, looking up from where she was placing the silverware by one of the plates. "Aggie got here extra early because she and I are going to take the pantry apart and clean it, and that's going to take some time."

"And what can I do while you do that?" Lily asked as she stepped over to get napkins from the cabinet.

"Why, I suppose you could begin your sewing business

full speed today," Ida May said with a grin, pointing to three large stacks of men's clothes. "Logan not only brought his mending and sewing, he brought Roy's and Ossie's as well."

Lily walked over to look at the clothes and said, "I do believe they have sent everything they own over here."

"It's all mending and hemming. I'll help you sort it all out. Logan explained everything," Ida May said. "And he said he'd be back by to take Violet to school since it's still muddy out there."

"Dear Logan thinks of everything," Lily said with appreciation in her voice. "As soon as breakfast is over, I'll begin work on the clothes. Are Aunt Janie Belle and Uncle Aaron feeling like coming downstairs today?"

"No, Janie Belle asked me to bring their breakfast upstairs. She said maybe up in the day sometime they'd come down," Ida May said with a frown. "I do hope they get to feeling better."

As soon as the meal was over, Logan came back to pick up Violet.

"It's right muddy and slippery out there yet," he told Lily. "I have to go into town, so I thought I'd check on y'all first and get Violet to school."

"Oh, thank you, Logan," Lily said. "Violet is ready to go. I'll go get her. And I have a letter to Aunt Emma if you would please mail it for me in town."

"Of course, I'd be glad to," Logan said.

As soon as Logan left with Violet and Lily's letter, Ida May asked Aggie to take trays up to Janie Belle and Aaron, and then she helped Lily carry the men's clothes into the new sewing room where a fire was already going in the fireplace. They placed them on a long table, and Ida May began sorting the garments.

"Now, these are Logan's," Ida May began, pushing some

pants to one side. "He has put pins in some of these pants for you to hem. He said he likes his work pants short enough to stay out of the dirt."

"These are Roy's," she continued, pushing another pile away. "His are mostly shirts, and they all need buttons. Then here's Ossie's. I believe he's written instructions." She pulled a piece of paper out of the pile and gave it to Lily.

Lily smiled and read the paper. "You're partly right," she said. "He also needs buttons on his brown suit, and he says the pants are just a fraction too long."

"Oh, dear, you need some buttons, don't you?" Ida May asked.

"No, I think I have enough. I found my button box. It's in the cabinet over there," Lily said, indicating the small piece of furniture with drawers in it at the other side of the room.

"Well, if you need more buttons or anything else, just come and let me know. Maybe I can help," Ida May said as she stepped away from the table. "Looks like you've got enough work to last awhile."

"Awhile, but not real long," Lily said, smiling at her. "I'm so used to doing this kind of work for Papa, I can float right through it."

By noontime Lily had accomplished a lot. All of Logan's were finished and most of Roy's when Ida May tapped on the door and told her Aggie had dinner on the table.

"Maybe I'll get a chance to talk to Aggie some time today," Lily said to herself as she laid aside the pants she was hemming and went to the kitchen.

As soon as the meal was finished, Ida May stood up and said, "Aggie, you go right ahead and clean up the table. I want to run some of this apple cobbler down to the Addisons. Mrs. Addison just loves this stuff." As she talked, she picked up a bowl from the cabinet and spooned the apple cobbler from the large pan on the cookstove.

"The Addisons?" Lily said, puzzled for a moment. "Oh, the people who live on Aunt Janie Belle's land."

"Yes, he more or less oversees the whole business of farming for your Uncle Aaron, since Aaron has become so old and feeble. I don't know what we'd do without the Addisons," Ida May said, continuing to fill the bowl.

"You know, the whole time I've been here, I haven't even seen them. It's almost like the farm runs itself," Lily remarked as she began stacking the dirty dishes.

"I sure wish it could," Ida May said, placing a clean dish towel over the bowl and setting it down by the door as she hastily put on her coat and hat. "I won't be long." She went on outside.

Now! Lily thought to herself. She and Aggie were alone.

"I don't know why Miz Ida May wants to give all dat away 'cause I'll jes' hafta make mo' tomorrow," Aggie fussed as she carried dirty dishes to the sink.

"Tomorrow is Saturday," Lily reminded her as she helped.

"Dat's right. You knows we has to always cook Sunday dinnuh on Sat'dy so de good Lawd won't git mad wid us fo' cookin' on Sundy," Aggie said.

"I know. I had just forgotten tomorrow will be Saturday," Lily said. She waited by the sink to dry the dishes as Aggie washed them. "Aggie, do you like working here? Really, honestly?"

"I sho' does," Aggie said firmly as she washed the plates. "Dis place be my home. I done tole you dat."

"I know," Lily said. She paused to look at the woman. "You know, Aggie, Logan told me about your papa getting killed and about my grandpa hiring your mother to work for Aunt Janie Belle and giving y'all a home here."

Aggie stopped to look at Lily and said, "Yo' grandpa didn't do no sech thing. Yo' Aunt Janie Belle, she hire my mama and tell us we kin come heah to live."

"Oh, but my grandpa was paying your mother her wages until he died," Lily explained. "Then Aunt Janie Belle began paying."

Aggie looked at her in great surprise and asked, "How come yo' grandpa do dat?"

"Because Grandpa wanted to do something for y'all. Your father worked for him for years and years, and then suddenly your mother was left alone with you to raise and Grandpa had plenty of money, so he paid."

Aggie scratched her head with a wet hand as she thought about it for a moment. "He wuz a good man, yo' grandpa wuz," she said. "I know he always he'pin' udder people."

"Yes, he was, Aggie. He was always helping other people, and I can't even get anyone to help me find out what happened to Grandpa's son, my papa," Lily said sadly as she looked at Aggie.

Aggie quickly turned back to washing the dishes, slopping the soapsuds in her hurry. "Jes' don't you be askin' me to he'p, 'cause I don't know nuthin' at all," she said. She reached to pull the dish towel out of Lily's hands. "I don't be needin' no he'p wid dese dishes. You jes' go back to yo' sewin' back dere."

Lily was surprised at the response she received.

"All right, Aggie," she said as she let Aggie have the dish towel. "But just remember, someday you're going to need help yourself about something, and it might be something important. Just don't come asking me for help."

She pretended to be angry with Aggie as she left the kitchen. She saw Aggie drop the dishrag into the dishpan and turn to look at her. But Lily ignored her.

When she got back to her sewing room, Lily began talking to herself.

"Hmmm! Logan's idea didn't work," Lily said aloud as she sat back down by the table and picked up the pants she had been hemming. "She wouldn't talk about those two strange men she saw with Papa, but she knew that's what I was wanting her to tell me about."

Lily's mind wandered as she looked at Ossie's clothes. He would be going to Charleston today, Friday, and his business dealings for Mr. Dutton didn't seem to take any set period of time, so she wouldn't expect him back until next week sometime at the earliest.

She wished she could just go to Charleston and roam around. Maybe if she inquired in shipping company offices, someone might remember her grandfather. He had been well known in the import-export business. But then there might be a hundred people with his surname operating through the port of Charleston, which was the largest in the Southeast.

Since Aggie was working that day, Lily didn't volunteer to help prepare dinner, but stuck right with her sewing. She only took time out to eat. She was fast, having had so much experience in the past few years. By the time Violet came home from school, she had almost finished Roy's clothes.

Violet opened the door just enough to call, "Lily, I'm home. I'm going outside with my puppy and kitten."

Lily looked up from where she was standing at the table folding clothes. "Wait, Violet," she said. "Did you walk on the road coming home, or did you cut through the fields and get all muddy?"

Violet stepped inside and twirled around. She had removed her cape. "I'm not dirty," she said. "I stayed on the road."

Lily could see she was clean. "All right, go ahead, but please don't get in mud out there," she said. "In fact, why don't you just play on the back porch?"

"But my puppy won't stay on the porch," Violet protested.

Lily stood up and said, "Come on. I'll show you how to block off the steps so he won't be able to get out so easily."

Lily went out on the back porch with Violet and picked up one of the large rocking chairs. "Here, you do it like this," she said as she tilted the rocker onto its side across the top of the steps. "Then you get another chair and lay it that way," she explained.

"But he can still get through the rockers," Violet said as she watched.

"I'm not finished yet," Lily said as she straightened up. "There's an old sheet in the pantry that we plan to tear up for rags. I'll get it."

Lily went back inside the kitchen. Aggie and Ida May were busy cleaning and scouring the cookstove.

"Aunt Ida May, do you mind if I use that old sheet in the pantry to help make a sort of barricade on the back porch so the puppy can't get out and Violet can play out there?" Lily asked.

"Of course. Go right ahead," Ida May said, looking up as she washed the inside of the oven. "And I might say that's a good idea to keep Violet out of that mud outside."

Returning to the back porch with sheet in hand, Lily finished blocking the steps to keep the puppy from getting out.

"What about my kitten?" Violet asked as she put the puppy down on the porch.

"There's no way we can stop him from going out, but if he gets muddy, he'll wash himself. The puppy won't," Lily explained. "Now, don't go anywhere else. And put on a jacket. It's chilly out here. I'll be in the sewing room if you need me."

Violet went to get a jacket and Lily went back to work.

Before Lily realized it, the day began to slip away, and she had to light the lamps in her sewing room. Soon she heard a knock on the sewing room door. "Come in," she called.

Aunt Ida May stepped into the room and looked at the sewing Lily had done.

"I just wanted to see if I could help out a little," her aunt said. "I already have the irons hot, so I could just press these hems and things for you."

Lily sighed and said, "Oh, thank you. I forgot all about that. If you could press Logan's clothes, I would have his all done."

"Of course, dear, just let me have them," Ida May said as she began picking up the stack belonging to Logan. "I'll have these done in no time."

"Thanks," Lily called to her as she left the room.

Aggie worked late on Fridays because of the general cleaning, so Lily did not have to help with the evening meal. When she went to eat, she noticed that Ida May had brought Violet and the animals inside and had dismantled the barricade on the porch by the time the food was on the table.

The meal finished, Lily had just returned to her sewing when there was a tap on the door of the sewing room. "Come in," Lily called.

She looked up to see Logan open the door. He stepped inside.

"I hate to interrupt such hard work, but I jes' wanted to thank you for what you've done to my clothes. I'll be settling up with you toward the end of the week," Logan said as he came to stand in front of the fireplace where logs were crackling away. "And I—"

"Settling up with me, my foot!" Lily interrupted as she stood up to stretch. "Remember this, Logan Garrett, there is no settling up to be done. And I don't want to hear any more about it."

"Well, you didn't let me finish," Logan protested as Lily came to join him in front of the warm fireplace.

Lily looked up at him and smiled. She said, "I'm sorry, Logan, but let's just don't talk about pay for the little mending I've done for you."

"All right, all right, but what I'm trying to tell you is that I found a window unlocked today in your papa's house," he said with a smile.

Lily gasped in delight. "Did you go inside?" she quickly asked.

"No, because Whitaker came riding up," Logan explained. "Roy and I were cleaning up after the rain. I was sweeping the water off the back porch and decided to try the windows and found one unlocked, but Whitaker came. He didn't go inside the house while we were there. He went down to the shed below the barn."

"I suppose with all the rain we've had, the barn must be in a wet mess since the roof was damaged by that fire we had while we were still living there," Lily said. "I'm just glad I didn't go into debt to get the barn redone."

"Yes, we had an awful lot of rain. It's standing everywhere in puddles."

"So when are you going inside the house?" Lily asked.

Logan scratched his head and said, "I don't rightly know."

"If you could just get inside and bring me my cloak and the key, then I could go back over there and finish looking around inside the house," Lily said.

"Well, I don't know about that," Logan replied. "If I just knew what you think you're looking for, I could do it for you when I get inside."

"Logan, I don't know what I'm looking for," Lily said. "There may be something we left behind, or there may be a secret hiding place of some kind."

"I jes' don't know how you're goin' to find something that you don't know you're looking for," Logan said as he added another log to the fire.

Lily laughed and said, "You make it sound complicated, but it's not really. First of all, I'm looking for anything I could see that might be in there that should have been moved out. Then I'll also be looking for hiding places where my mother could have kept her jewelry and other valuables that she wrote about in her letter." She sat down on a stool in front of the fire.

"In that case," he said, perching on the corner of the long table, "let me do the first looking. If I see anything that belongs to you that was left in the house, I'll get it out somehow and bring it to you. Because whatever it would be, it would not belong to Whitaker. He only bought the house, not the contents."

"That's right," Lily agreed. "If I find anything that's mine, he can't claim it. When do you plan on going back?"

"Well, jes' as soon as I can get a chance," Logan said. "I'll have to pick my chance and at least pretend to be busy working around there doing something."

Lily remembered her conversation with Aggie and changed the subject.

"Your idea didn't work with Aggie," she said, explaining what had transpired between the two of them earlier that day. "It may be a bad thing for me to say, but I hope Aggie needs something or someone and she has to ask me."

"You know Aggie. She's a big pretender," Logan said

with a smile. "Give her time. She doesn't like to be rushed. She'll come across one day."

"Well, I sure hope she doesn't take too much time doing it," Lily said with a deep sigh. "She might have information that would help solve the mystery of my papa's death."

Lily gazed into the burning logs as she thought about the sudden death of her father. She would never accept the conclusion of the sheriff that he had died from an accident while shoeing a horse. He had been too expert a blacksmith for that to ever happen.

Logan was silent also for a moment, and then he said, "You know, Whitaker has never been seen going near your papa's shop since he bought the place. As far as I can tell, it's been closed up all this time, and no one has bothered it."

"Well, I don't understand what he wanted with our property anyway," Lily said with a deep frown. "At first I thought he wanted to move into our house, but he hasn't so far. And you'd think he would repair the barn instead of letting it stand there and get damaged with all this rain and the roof mostly gone."

"I understand he's a tightwad," Logan said. "There's been talk around town about him wanting to do business with local merchants and trying to cheat them. Then I heard that he had bought up some businesses just to show his power."

"Logan, I know it's too late today, but please try to get inside the house tomorrow before the man finds my cloak and the key in the pocket," Lily urged him. "Do you want me to come and stand somewhere as a lookout? If I saw him coming, I could run and let you know."

"No, no, no!" Logan said emphatically. "I don't want you involved in this. I'll see what I can do, maybe tomorrow."

"Will you come by here as soon as you do go inside the house? Please," Lily asked anxiously.

Logan smiled at her and said, "Of course, I'll come and let you know just as soon as I'm able to get inside and find out whether there's anything in there belonging to you."

"Thanks, Logan," Lily said. "And I appreciate your mailing that letter for me to Aunt Emma. Maybe she'll have some information to give me when she writes back, which will take a long time from England."

"Right now you have lots of irons in the fire, but one day soon you'll be able to sort it all out," Logan told her. "It'll all come together somehow."

"If Aunt Janie Belle or Uncle Aaron could just remember the name of the man my father went to see in Charleston, that might be the beginning of the solution to a lot of these things," Lily said, looking up at Logan.

"You're right," said Logan, "but right now you need to work with what you've got." He moved to the door and said, "I've got to go. Maybe I'll be seein' you tomorrow."

"Bye," she said, and closed the door behind him before she returned to her sewing.

When Lily went to bed that night, she couldn't sleep soundly because of all the problems nagging at her mind. She felt like something big was about to explode, and she couldn't decide whether it would be good or bad.

Chapter Ten
Aggie Helps

Aggie came back the next morning. She and Ida May would be cooking almost all day for the next day's dinner.

Janie Belle and Aaron were still staying in their rooms and were not planning to eat downstairs anytime soon. "I got permission from your Aunt Janie Belle to ask Logan and Roy to have dinner with us tomorrow. Ossie has gone to Charleston, and Logan is alone anyway," Ida May explained after she had taken the breakfast tray upstairs to her sister and brother-in-law.

"I'm sure they'll both be thankful for a good meal," Lily said as she pressed the clothes she had mended the night before.

Ida May pushed the chairs back in place around the table after Aggie had cleared it off. She stopped and looked at Lily as she asked, "Do you feel like going to church tomorrow with me?"

Lily cringed as she thought about having to face outsiders and deal with their sympathy for her father's death.

Because of that, she had not been able to attend church since she had come home. On Sundays, while everyone went, she had been reading from the Bible to Violet and teaching her a lesson, and the minister had dropped by several times.

"I'm sorry, but I just need more time. Everyone will be asking questions and extending sympathy, and I just can't stand up to that yet," Lily told her.

"I understand, dear. Just let me know when you feel like you're ready to go," Ida May replied. She went over to the stove and opened the oven door to check a hen she was baking.

Aggie was washing dishes, and she glanced at Lily out of the corner of her eye, but remained silent.

The day was warm and the sun was shining. The ground had dried enough that Lily had allowed Violet to play outside with her pets. Lily looked out the window to be sure the child was still there. She saw Violet running up and down the walkway with the puppy at her heels. The white kitten sat on the banister of the porch and watched.

"I hate to see cold weather come because Violet can't play outdoors," Lily remarked as she went back to her ironing. "Especially since she doesn't have anywhere in the house to play except here in the kitchen, and when Aunt Janie Belle and Uncle Aaron get able to come back downstairs, I'm afraid she'll irritate them."

Ida May straightened up from the stove to look at her. "Why, there are lots of rooms in this house that are not being used," she said. "Why couldn't we convert one of them into a playroom for the child?"

Lily brightened up at the idea, but then she had second thoughts. "But that would mean we'd have to have a fire going in the room, and that would cost Aunt Janie Belle money," she said.

"Money? Not if we could prevail upon Logan or Roy to keep the wood chopped and brought in," Ida May said. "That way it wouldn't be added to the duties of the Addisons. Janie Belle doesn't like them coming in the house anyway."

"I'm sure either one of them, Logan or Roy, would be glad to look after the wood, but I'd hate to ask them," Lily said as she folded a shirt that she had mended.

"Oh, Lily, don't think like that," Ida May said as she walked across to embrace Lily. "We all love you and Violet, and it's a pleasure for Logan and Roy to do things for y'all. You ought to realize that. Just leave it to me. I'll do all the asking."

"Do you think Aunt Janie Belle will allow it?" Lily asked.

"Of course," Aunt Ida May said as she went back to the stove to check on the contents of a pot. "And I know the very room—the one right next to your sewing room would be ideal."

"But that's the little bedroom that you just made curtains for," Lily said.

"Which means we'll have new curtains for the room," Ida May said. "I'll get Roy and Logan to put the bedroom furniture up into the attic."

"In the attic?" Lily questions. "Don't you ever have company using that room?"

"No, not in a long, long time, and we'd have to have lots of company to get around to using that bedroom," Ida May said as she checked the hen in the oven again. "There are two other bedrooms beyond that one on this floor and all those others upstairs."

At that moment, they heard a knock on the back door. Lily went and opened it. Logan was there, and she became excited when she saw he was carrying her cloak.

"Come on in," she told him. She reached for the cloak as he stepped inside.

Logan let her take it, and Lily quickly stuck her hand into the pocket and brought out the key to her father's house. She hung the cloak on a peg by the door before her aunt noticed.

"Mornin', Miss Ida May," Logan greeted the lady as she wiped her hands on her apron and turned to greet him.

"Good morning to you, Logan," Ida May said, pushing back a stray lock of dark hair. "You don't know it, but you just walked into another mess of work."

"What can I do for y'all?" he asked.

Lily was eager to ask questions but didn't want to in front of her aunt, and especially with Aggie around.

"We need a room emptied out so we can make it into a playroom for Violet," Ida May explained.

Lily quickly spoke up. "I'll show him where it is," she said. "Come on this way, Logan." She started toward the hall door.

Logan followed Lily down the hallway to the doorway of the little bedroom, and she paused there to ask, "Did you find anything inside the house?"

Logan shook his head as he replied, "No, not a thing. I looked in every room and didn't see anything of any shape or form. We must have got every little thing out when we moved y'all over here."

"Then I have to go back and look for some secret hiding place," Lily said, disappointed. "There has just got to be something somewhere." She frowned as she thought about it.

"I checked everywhere and I couldn't find anything," he said. And then grinning, he added, "I even searched for secret hiding places like you've been talking about, but I didn't really expect to find such a thing."

"Logan, you know how old that house is," Lily said. "It was built way back in the days when people had secret places to hide things. I'd like to go over there while everyone's at church tomorrow, but I'll have Violet here and I can't go then."

"That time wouldn't be too good anyway," Logan said. "I have to go to church tomorrow and I don't want you over there unless I'm with you."

"Oh, you and Roy are invited to dinner here after church," Lily said as she pushed open the door to the little bedroom. "Aunt Ida May said Aunt Janie Belle allowed her to invite y'all."

Logan looked at her, puzzled. "Something special going on?" he asked.

"No, it's just that Aunt Janie Belle and Uncle Aaron are still not able to come downstairs. Aunt Ida May and Violet and I will be alone, and Roy is alone because Ossie has gone to Charleston, and you're alone, as far as we know," Lily explained as she stopped to take a breath.

"Well, I thank you. I'll be here as soon as I can get from church," he said.

"Oh, but you have to let Aunt Ida May invite you, and don't let her know I did, because this is not my house, understand?" Lily said with a big grin.

"If you say so. I'll act real surprised when she does," Logan said, grinning back. "Now, what is it you want me and Roy to do here?"

Lily waved her hands around the room. "Take all this furniture up to the attic," she said. "And this was Aunt Ida May's idea, too, not mine. She has to get permission from Aunt Janie Belle before you and Roy can move it."

"So that makes it about Monday before we can get this done then," Logan said as he walked around, looking at the furniture.

"I suppose," Lily said. "We are going to make this a playroom for Violet. You all could do it whenever you have time."

"I'll speak to Roy on my way home," Logan said. "And I need to be headin' on home, too." He started out the door.

"Wait," Lily said quickly. "I can't talk about what I'm planning in front of Aunt Ida May. If you insist on going back to Papa's house with me, when will you be able to go?"

Logan stopped to scratch his head as he replied, "I'll have to let you know, 'cause I jes' don't know right now. Probably be Monday."

"Please don't make me wait long," Lily begged.

"Probably Monday," Logan repeated as they walked back down the hallway to the kitchen.

Lily looked around the room. Ida May was not there.

"Did Aunt Ida May go out somewhere, Aggie?" Lily asked the woman, who was now drying her hands at the sink.

Aggie turned to look at her and said, "She took coffee up to Miz Janie Belle."

Lily went over to the stove to lift a pot lid and look inside. "I believe these beans need some water," she said, mostly to herself.

But Aggie thought she was talking to her. "Den you put de watuh in de beans," she said. "I'se got to talk wid Mistuh Logan 'fo he go." She motioned to Logan to follow her out the back door.

Logan winked at Lily and stepped outside onto the porch. Aggie reached back to pull the door shut, but Lily noticed it didn't quite close.

Lily could hear Aggie saying, "Mistuh Logan, dat Miz Lily she think I knows somethin' 'bout her pa's death, but I don't. I sho' don't know nuthin'."

"I'm sorry to hear that, Aggie," Lily heard Logan reply. "Because I was hopin' you could help us find out what happened to Miss Lily's papa. You see, we don't believe a horse killed him like the sheriff said."

"Oh, no, Mistuh Logan, no hoss didn't kill po' Mistuh Charlie, no sirree," she said."

"How do you know that, Aggie? Did you see what happened that day?" Logan asked.

"Lawsy mercy, Mistuh Logan, I don't know nuthin', I don't," she said. "All I knows is I saw strange men. Dey didn't look like nobody 'round heah."

"Stop and think about this, Aggie," Logan replied. "If you know anything at all, you should tell Miss Lily, or tell me if you don't want to talk to her about it. If those two men were strangers and don't live around here, we need to find out who they were. What did they look like?"

"Dey jes' look like two strange men, they do," Aggie insisted.

"When you saw them, what were they doing?" Logan asked.

"Oh, Mistuh Logan, dey shoutin', yellin', and bein' real loud," Aggie replied.

Lily, listening in the kitchen, realized Aggie was not telling Logan much more than what she had told her.

"Was there anyone else down there?" Logan asked.

"No, jes' dem two strange men and Mistuh Charlie. Po' Mistuh Charlie, he wuz a good man, he wuz," Aggie said in a sad voice.

"Yes, he was, and that's the reason you need to tell us everything you can remember about that morning—what you saw down at the blacksmith shop," Logan told her. "Would you know those men if you saw them again?"

Aggie hesitated before she answered. Then she said

quickly, "I don't think so. No, I wouldn't. Ain't seed 'em since and don't 'spect to."

"Remember, Aggie, Mister Charlie was Mister Tad's son, the only living son he had, and Mister Tad did right by your own pa, remember?" Logan told her.

Aggie was silent, and Logan continued, "Whoever killed Mister Charlie needs to be brought in by the law and made to stand trial for it. It's not right that someone can kill another man like that and get away with it. That person might just go out and kill somebody else."

"Lawsy mercy, Mistuh Logan, dat's whut my Tinny tell me. Dem men might kill us, we mess in dere business," Aggie said, almost in tears.

"But they wouldn't be able to kill you if the law brought them in and put them in jail and tried them," Logan said.

Lily was thinking Aggie probably did know something, and whatever it was, she was too afraid to tell, either from fear of the strange men or from fear of her husband.

"But dey might git out, too," Aggie said. "No, I don't know nuthin', nuthin' atall."

"I've got to go now, Aggie, but you think about all this and you come and talk to me when you decide to tell whatever you know about those strange men," Logan said.

"I gotta go back to work, too," Aggie told him.

Lily rushed away from the door as Aggie pushed it open and came back into the kitchen. The woman went directly to the sink and began on another stack of dirty dishes.

Logan stuck his head back inside the door, retrieved his hat from the peg, and said, "See y'all later."

At that moment, Ida May came into the kitchen from the hallway. "Wait," she called to Logan.

She hurried across the room as Logan paused in the doorway.

"Please ask Roy for me," she told him. "We would like

for you and Roy to come have dinner with us after church tomorrow if you don't have other plans."

"Yes, ma'am, I mean no, ma'am, I don't have any plans, and I thank you, Miss Ida May," Logan said with a big smile as he glanced toward Lily. "And I'll stop by and tell Roy on the way home. I was going to see him anyway about moving that furniture out of that bedroom for y'all."

"We would appreciate that, Logan," Ida May said, smiling at him. "And we'll look for both of you to come on over here straight from church."

"Yes, ma'am, Miss Ida May, we'll be here," Logan said, and waving to Lily, he closed the door behind him as he left the kitchen.

"Logan said they could probably move the stuff Monday," Lily told her as she finished folding the clothes she had ironed. She glanced at Aggie. The woman was furiously washing the dishes.

"That will be fine," Ida May said. She went back to check things on the stove again.

Lily suddenly realized she didn't hear Violet outside. She hurried to the window and looked into the yard. There was no sign of her or the puppy.

"Violet!" she exclaimed as she ran to throw open the door and rush out onto the porch.

"What is it?" Ida May cried, following right behind her.

"She's not here!" Lily ran into the yard calling the child's name, "Violet! Violet! Where are you, Violet?"

Ida May followed and began running around the yard, looking behind bushes. "Violet! Come here, Violet!"

Lily ran around the house, then circled back and rushed down to the barn. "Violet! Violet!" she cried as she raced through the building in search of her little sister.

Lily's horse, Lightnin', heard all the commotion, came up to the fence behind the barn, and began whinnying. Lily paused long enough to rub his head as her eyes searched the pasture behind him.

"Violet, where are you? Answer me!" Lily called as loudly as she could.

"I'm going to look out on the road," Ida May yelled at her. She hurried down the driveway out of the yard.

"I'll go this way," Lily yelled back at her as she motioned toward the pathway to the springhouse.

Ida May disappeared around the curve, and Lily turned and started in the other direction. She was going so fast, she almost fell as Violet's white puppy came running to meet her. He was crying as though he was lost.

"Where is Violet?" Lily asked, looking down at the puppy. She continued on her way and the puppy turned and ran ahead of her. He looked back to see if she was following.

Lily came within sight of the springhouse and spotted her little sister lying on the grass near it.

"Violet, Violet," she cried as she ran to her. Violet was crying.

As Lily reached down to touch her, Violet suddenly sat up, and Lily could see that she was muddy all over. She stooped down to look at the child.

"Violet, are you all right?" Lily asked. She reached to take her into her arms. "Why didn't you answer me? I know you could hear me calling you. You had me worried, and Aunt Ida May has gone out to the road looking for you."

Violet pulled away from her and said in a shaky voice, "I'm all dirty because I fell down and hurt my foot."

Lily quickly felt for her feet. "You hurt your foot? Which one?" she asked.

"That one," Violet said, pointing at the right one.

Lily just barely touched her right foot and Violet jerked it away. "You hurt me! You hurt me!" she cried.

"Violet, we've got to get you to the house," Lily said. "Logan just left, so I suppose I'll have to carry you if you can't walk. Here, let me help you up. Stand up on your good foot. Don't put any weight on the hurt foot."

As Lily supported her, Violet stood up on her left foot.

"Now, put your arm around me and I'll pick you up," Lily instructed the child.

"No, you won't either, Miz Lily," Aggie said suddenly behind her. "Heah, lemme git hold of dat chile."

Before Lily could turn and protest, Aggie had swung Violet up into her arms and had started toward the house. Lily followed.

"You po' baby," Aggie was talking to Violet as they went along. "Done hurt yo' po' lil foot. Well, we fix dat."

As they neared the house, Lily saw Ida May returning from the road. Lily waved at her to get her attention. Her aunt saw them and got to the back door just as they did.

"My puppy!" Violet said as Aggie started through the back door.

Lily quickly looked around, saw the puppy right behind them, and said, "Here he is. We'll let him into the house." She held the door open, and the little animal hurried into the kitchen and headed for the warmth of the cookstove.

Aggie laid Violet on the table where Lily had been ironing. She stepped over to the sink to get a pan of water and a washcloth. "We'se got to clean you up 'fo we can see what de matter be," she said, hurrying as she talked.

"Is she hurt?" Ida May asked.

"She said she hurt her foot, the right one. Could you look at it for me and see what you think?" Lily said under her breath to her aunt.

Ida May moved forward and touched Violet's right foot. Violet jerked it away.

"I'm not going to hurt you, dear," Aunt Ida May told her. "Just let me look at it so we'll know what's wrong with it. Then we can doctor it up real good." She reached toward it again and Violet moved it again.

"Heah, let old Aggie see 'bout it," the woman said as she quickly pulled Violet's right cotton stocking down and off the foot before the child knew what was happening. "Aha, it ain't nuthin' but a scratch. You musta skint it on sumpin'," she continued.

Lily and Ida May hovered over her, watching.

"Is that all that's wrong with it, Aggie?" Lily asked.

Aggie was carefully feeling along the large scratch on the ankle. Violet was lying still, but she was looking at every move. The woman glanced up at Lily, smiled, and said, "Jes' like I done said, ain't nuthin' but a scratch, and we kin bathe most of dat away." She began washing the foot. Violet winced a little but allowed her to do it.

"It's not broken?" Violet asked.

"No, dat thang ain't broken," Aggie said, with a big smile as she finished cleaning the mud off Violet. Lily got clean clothes from Violet's room. Once she was dressed, Violet was all right. She didn't even limp when Aggie stood her on the floor.

"You see, you kin walk all right," Aggie told her as she watched Violet put both feet on the floor.

Violet looked down at her feet and said with a catch in her voice, "I thought it broke. And I was afraid you'd be mad at me, Lily."

Lily put an arm around her as she replied, "I'm not mad at you, dear. You had me worried to death just about. You didn't answer when I called for you. Didn't you hear me?"

"I heard you. I sent my puppy up to the house to get

you," Violet said, looking over at the puppy curled up by the stove.

Lily sighed and looked at the other two women. Standing over Violet, the three of them smiled.

Violet sat down in a chair, and looking up at Ida May, she asked, "Are you mad at me?"

"Me? Why no, dear. I was just worried like your sister here," Ida May replied. "Why do you ask?"

"I was afraid you'd be mad at me, Aunt Ida May, and I wouldn't get to go to church with you tomorrow," Violet said, hurriedly looking around at Lily.

Ida May answered, "You want to go to church with me tomorrow, then you'll go. I'll be proud to have your company—such a pretty little girl."

Lily was relieved that Violet had finally decided on her own that she wanted to go back to church. But she herself just couldn't make it yet. Maybe the next Sunday.

Then Lily remembered Aggie's kindness and she turned to the woman. "Aggie, I appreciate what you've done for Violet," she said. "I thank you from the bottom of my heart." She smiled at Aggie.

The woman turned away toward the stove and she said, grumbling, "Ain't nuthin' to be thankin' me fo'." She noisily moved pots and pans about on the stove.

"Is all the food about done, Aggie?" Ida May asked as she went to look inside the pots.

"Jes' 'bout," Aggie replied.

"Get the bowls and things, Aggie, and dip out enough of everything for you to take home for y'all's dinner tomorrow," Ida May told her.

"Yessum," the woman said as she went into the pantry.

Lily was still hovering over Violet in the chair, but she was also listening to the conversation. Aggie really was a good woman at heart.

Chapter Eleven
Broken Promises

Sunday morning after breakfast, Lily helped Violet dress. She had pressed her little sister's favorite dress, white with pink rosebuds embroidered on the full skirt hem and the matching bonnet. Violet was excited because she was going to church with Aunt Ida May.

"How is your foot this morning?" Lily asked as she watched Violet pull on her cotton stockings over the scratch.

Violet paused to look at her ankle and said, "It's all right. I forgot all about it."

Lily smiled and then said, "Now, I want you to be sure your pets are out of the house when you leave. I don't want Aunt Janie Belle coming downstairs and finding them."

"I've already put them on the back porch," Violet told her. "Is Aunt Janie Belle well now?"

"No, she and Uncle Aaron are old," Lily explained. "And when you get old, sometimes you get pains in your joints—like your knees and wrists—and they've been resting in their rooms this week. Aunt Ida May said they would not be down today. Remember, Logan and Roy are coming to eat dinner with us."

"I've got to go, Lily," Violet protested. "Aunt Ida May might leave me."

Lily smiled and said, "No danger of that." She quickly tied the ribbons to hold on Violet's bonnet.

They went downstairs, and Ida May and Violet left in Aunt Janie Belle's buggy. Lily watched from the back porch.

"I'll have everything ready for dinner when y'all get back," Lily promised as they drove off.

Lily went back inside the house and looked around the long kitchen. She could go ahead and set the table and have that much done. Going to the cabinet, she took out the china and silverware and started toward the table.

"Aunt Ida May didn't say whether we are going to eat here in the kitchen or in the dining room," she said to herself, pausing with a load of dishes in her hands. Then she decided. "Let's eat in the dining room. After all, today is Sunday and everyone will be dressed up."

She went on into the dining room and saw that someone had already started the fire in the huge rock fireplace— probably Mr. Addison. He seemed to always be doing things without anyone seeing him. Ida May would have asked him to do this, Lily reasoned, so she must have been planning to eat in the dining room.

Setting the dishes on the sideboard, she opened a drawer, took out a long white linen tablecloth, shook it out, and spread it on the table. She set places for five people— Roy, Logan, Ida May, Violet, and herself.

Standing back to survey her work, she said to herself, "Now that's done. But it's too early to warm the food."

What was she going to do with herself until Violet and Aunt Ida May returned from church? Ordinarily she would be reading the Bible to her little sister during church hours, but Violet was gone today.

When she came back into the kitchen, she glanced at her cloak still hanging on one of the pegs by the door, and she knew at once what she would do with her time.

Taking the stairs two at a time, quietly so as not to disturb Aunt Janie Belle and Uncle Aaron, Lily rushed up to her room. She picked up the key to her father's house from her bureau, went back downstairs, and put on the cloak.

"I'll just go look around," she said to herself as she went out the back door and softly closed it.

The weather was chilly, but the sun was shining and the mud was gone. So Lily decided to walk as she had done many times before when she still lived in her father's house. She cut across fields and came out on the road near where she had fallen into the drainage ditch before.

"I'm not taking a chance on that again," Lily muttered to herself, and she continued walking on the road until she came to a pathway across the ditch under which a pipe had been laid. Lifting her long skirts, she hurried up the path, which was overgrown with weeds and briars. She was now on what had been her father's old property, but she couldn't see the house because of thick bushes and trees growing around her.

Just as she stepped into the clearing at the back of the house, she happened to glance ahead and saw a movement down near the barn. Darting behind the bushes, she watched to see who or what it was. Mr. Whitaker was coming up the path from the barn. He was leading his horse and looking in the other direction. He kept turning to glance behind him.

"Oh!" she exclaimed to herself. "If he sees me, I'm in trouble!" Her heart was racing so hard, it shook her body.

Her face and hands felt like they were on fire. She felt perspiration drip down her arms, under her sleeves.

When Mr. Whitaker got up to the driveway, he stopped and mounted his horse. He sat there a few minutes, gazing around the area. Lily shrank behind the bushes and could see only through a tiny opening. Finally the man shook the reins, and his horse galloped on up the driveway toward the road.

Lily listened until the horse's hoofs died away in the distance before she took a deep breath and stepped out into the clearing again. Her hand grasped the key in her pocket. Mr. Whitaker was gone. She was going into the house.

She paused to listen and look around again when she reached the back porch, just to be sure there was no one else on the property. Then she inserted the big key, turned the lock, pushed open the door, stepped inside with a huge sigh, and closed it behind her. Quickly removing her cloak, she hung it on the peg where she had left it before. But this time, when she locked the door from the inside, she put the key in the pocket of her skirt.

"Logan has searched everywhere that he could think of," she said to herself. "I'd think a hiding place would probably be in a closet. And I think I'll begin upstairs."

Going all the way to the end of the hallway upstairs, Lily began searching the closets in every room. There weren't very many because they had used huge wardrobes to hold their clothes. Today the sun was shining so she could see fairly well inside as she pushed on walls and tapped on door facings.

"Nothing," she said in a disappointed voice as she finished the last room, which had been her mother's. "Nothing."

Finally she stood by the fireplace, trying to decide what to do next. Suddenly she heard horse's hoofs outside. She peeked out the window to the front yard and saw Wilbur Whitaker riding up on his horse. As he disappeared around the side of the house, Lily turned, intending to run across the hallway and look down into the backyard to see where he went.

Her heavy skirts hindered her from moving quickly, and her foot slipped on the polished hardwood floor, causing her to lose her balance. She grabbed for the corner of the mantelpiece, missed it, and fell against the built-in bookcase next to it.

The bookcase gave away and she kept falling and falling, unable to reach anything to stop. Finally she landed with a bang. The bookcase had opened up and she was now behind it, but it had closed behind her again. It was too dark to see where she was.

How will I ever get out of here? was the first thing that came to her mind. She stood up and began feeling around the walls. She seemed to be in a space about four feet wide and six or eight feet long, probably the size of the bookcase that had covered it.

Remembering that Wilbur was in the yard, she became still and kept listening for him. But she couldn't hear a sound. Either the enclosure was soundproof, or there was no one in the house.

"I've got to get out," she exclaimed as she once again began examining the walls. They seemed to be smooth, finished wood without any hinge or attachment to open the bookcase.

Then suddenly the bookcase swung open, and she had no idea how it had happened. She must have touched something, she guessed. Holding the bookcase as she stepped back into the room, she peered inside the secret space and immediately saw a panel on the wall that had slid halfway open, revealing a small door.

"Just what I was looking for!" she exclaimed as she tried to reach it with one hand while still keeping her hold on the bookcase with the other. The distance was too great. She needed something to prop against the bookcase to keep it from closing while she examined the hidden door.

"What, what, what?" she muttered to herself as she tried to think of something in the house to use, but then she realized she would have to let go of the bookcase if she went looking for something, and the bookcase would close. She might never be able to get it open again. There was no visible catch to push or turn to operate it.

At that moment she heard the echo in the empty house of someone turning the key in the lock in the kitchen door downstairs. Her heart thumped wildly as she tried to think what to do.

"I'll just get back inside," she decided to herself. And as she stepped back into the hiding space she reached down, removed one of her shoes, and stuck it behind the bookcase as it closed, leaving a tiny opening.

"I don't know how much out of place the bookcase is on the other side, but maybe if someone comes in here, he or she won't notice," she mumbled to herself as she listened for footsteps. There was only silence.

Suddenly someone began whistling a song, and she knew it must be Wilbur. She heard the sound of doors being opened and slammed shut as the whistling continued. Then there were heavy footsteps coming up the stairway nearby.

"Dear God, please, please, don't let him find me," she cried under her breath.

She was afraid of this young man alone with her in an empty house. He had seemed interested in her while they were on the ship coming home from England, and she had been attracted to him. But he seemed to blow hot and cold. His attitude seemed to change with nothing to cause it.

The day he had found her in the ditch he had insisted that he wanted to talk to her, but she had been so upset, she didn't pay attention to whatever he was trying to say. She could only think about getting away from him. And if Logan had not come by and rescued her, there was no telling what might have happened because Wilbur seemed intent on helping her one way or another.

The footsteps paused at the top of the stairs, and then Lily heard them go down the hallway in the opposite direction from where she was. The whistling persisted as Wilbur continued opening and slamming doors.

In a few minutes, the footsteps came back down the hallway in her direction, and the opening and closing of doors continued as evidently he came back up the hallway from that end.

Then all sound ceased. Lily held her breath. Where was he? Outside the door of the room she was in? Or in the room itself?

Her question was answered as Wilbur's voice called out loudly, "Where are you? I know you're in this house because I saw you come in. Lily? Where are you?" He must be in the doorway of the room.

Lily wondered whether she dared pull her shoe inside and cause the bookcase to close. But that might make a noise, and she didn't want Wilbur Whitaker to know of the secret hiding place, especially since she had not yet explored the small door in the wall. So she stood completely still and tried to hold her breath.

Finally, after what seemed hours, she heard Wilbur walk into the hallway, all the time calling her name, "Lily! Lily! Where are you? I just want to talk to you . . . about something really important. Lily, please quit evading me."

Apparently he thought she was in the house and was able to dart from room to room to hide from him.

Then she heard him starting up the creaky steps to the attic. Did she dare try to leave while he was up there? No, she decided she couldn't leave. She had not had time to open the small door yet, and she just had to know what was behind that little door. So she continued standing still and silent.

In a few moments she heard Wilbur tramping overhead across the attic floor, still calling, "Lily! Lily!"

When would he give up and go away? The air inside the small space was becoming hot and stuffy, and she didn't know how much longer she could stay where she was.

Suddenly she heard horse's hoofs in the yard, and she knew it could not be Wilbur on his horse. Evidently he had heard the horse, because his footsteps stopped as though he were listening, too.

In a few moments, Lily heard the echo of the key turning in the back door, the door opening and then closing. Footsteps came along the downstairs hallway.

Lily's heart beat wildly as she heard the footsteps continue up the staircase and come down the hallway. She couldn't see, but they seemed to pause outside the doorway of the room where she was hiding.

There was total silence in the house for a few minutes, which seemed like hours. Whoever had come in must be still standing in the hallway outside her mother's room. Then she heard the creak of the door to the hallway. The door never stayed all the way open, and she knew the sound from having pushed it open so many times herself.

The person was coming into the room. She held her breath and froze. Suddenly there was a loud commotion and the sound of a blow followed by a few grunts. Then evidently someone fell to the floor. It scared her so much she accidentally bumped into the back of the bookcase and caused it to swing open.

She saw Mr. Whitaker lying on the floor and Wilbur bending over him. He looked up and caught a glimpse of Lily as she tried to withdraw into the secret hiding space, but he was too quick on his feet and had reached the bookcase before she could close it.

"Lily," he said as he stood there holding the bookcase open and staring down at her. "Why didn't you answer me when I called you?"

"Wilbur, what do you want?" Lily said, finally stepping out into the room and bending to retrieve her shoe from where it had held the bookcase open.

"I've been trying to catch up with you for days," he said.

Lily glanced at Mr. Whitaker again. He was out cold.

"Why did you knock out your father?" she asked as she tried to move toward the hallway. Wilbur kept maneuvering between her and the door.

"Wait, Lily," he said. "I had to knock him out to keep him from finding you in the house."

Lily frowned and stopped to look up at the handsome man.

"What difference does that make to you? After all, he's your father," Lily replied as she tried to put her shoe back on while standing on the other foot.

"It makes a lot of difference, because I don't think he always plays fair and I know for a fact he would put you in jail if he caught you in this house," Wilbur told her.

Lily almost had her shoe on, then suddenly she lost her balance and sat down in front of Wilbur.

"Here, let me help you," Wilbur said as he stooped to assist her in putting on the shoe. "What were you doing with a shoe off anyway?" He managed to push it onto her foot. Lily fastened it and stood up.

"Wilbur, I've got to go," she said, anxiously looking at

Mr. Whitaker lying on the floor. "Will your father be all right?"

"Oh, sure, this has happened before," Wilbur told her as he stepped in front of her. "Ever since I got old enough and big enough to fight back."

Lily looked at him in surprise. "Why do you fight with your father?" she asked.

"Because I don't always agree with the things he does," Wilbur said. "And what I'm getting around to is—there's something in this house that belongs to you and I didn't want my father to find it."

Lily's blue eyes opened in surprise as she looked up at him.

"What are you talking about?" she asked.

"Here, I'll show you," Wilbur said. He walked over to the bookcase and pushed on the end of it, and it swung open. He then tripped a catch at the other end to make it stay open.

Lily watched in amazement. Wilbur seemed to know everything about the secret place.

Wilbur stepped inside the small room and Lily followed him. "Now, look in there," Wilbur said as he caught her hand and pointed inside. "There's a small door on the back wall, and do you know what's on the other side of the door?"

Lily was shocked into silence as she stared at Wilbur opening the door and pulling out a metal box and a brocade bag.

"Here, these belong to you," Wilbur said. He brought the items out into the room and handed them to her.

Lily took them hesitantly and then sat down on the floor. She eagerly opened the metal box while Wilbur stooped nearby watching. It was full of papers, what looked like legal papers. She closed it and opened the bag. She began to cry as her fingers pulled out her mother's jewels—every color, every shape, and size.

Wilbur took a handkerchief from his pocket and handed it to her. "Don't cry," he said. "You should be happy that I found these things before my father or someone else did. You would never have seen them then."

Lily kept crying in spite of herself, and Wilbur sat down beside her on the floor. When he did, she reached to squeeze his hand.

"Thank you," she tried to say.

Wilbur squeezed her hand and said, "You've got to put these in the bag and get out of this house, Lily. My father will wake up any minute now."

He helped her put the contents back into the bag, and together they stood up. Wilbur took the metal box and led her down the stairs. Lily carried the bag containing the jewelry.

"Wilbur, I appreciate this," she said in a shaky voice as she shifted the heavy bag to her other hand.

"Come on, I'm going to take you home, and I have to get away from here before my father wakes up and finds out who it was that knocked him out," Wilbur told her as he opened the back door with his key.

Lily remembered to snatch her cloak from the peg and followed him out onto the back porch. He locked the door and led her around the house to his horse he had hidden behind some bushes.

"Come on," he urged her. "Step up on the block and give me your hand." He mounted his horse and reached to swing her up.

Lily was speechless with surprise at Wilbur's attitude and the discovery of her mother's jewelry. When he stopped his horse by the mounting block at Aunt Janie Belle's house, he jumped down, then reached up for the box and the bag, set them on the ground, and lifted Lily down to her feet.

Lily reached to squeeze his hand again. "I thank you with all my heart, Wilbur," she said. "I'll always remember this, and I'll always be grateful."

"Well, while you're remembering, don't forget about me. I'll be back soon," he told her as he remounted and galloped off on his horse.

Lily felt as though things were not quite real as she picked up the metal box and the bag and carried them up to her room. She dumped the contents of the bag onto the counterpane on her bed. The pieces were dazzling. She had no idea whether they were real jewels or not, but they had belonged to her mother and she caressed each piece as she examined it. And there in a little velvet bag she found the broken pearl necklace Aunt Janie Belle had talked about. It was originally three strands, as Ida May had said, and the third string was still broken with the loose pearls lying inside.

"Oh, Mother, Mother!" she cried as her blue eyes flooded with tears again and she reached for her handkerchief to wipe them. With tear-blurred vision, she glanced at the monogram on it and saw a large *W* embroidered in white thread. Suddenly she realized it belonged to Wilbur. She had forgotten to return it to him.

She crawled up on the bed and sat down as she thought about Wilbur. What was he up to? He could have taken the jewelry himself, and she would never have known it even existed. But instead he had guarded it for her against his own father. He was indeed a strange man. And he had said he would be back. What was she to do about him?

Suddenly she heard voices downstairs and realized everyone had come from church and she had not even heard the horses outside. Returning the jewelry to the brocade bag, she fastened it and looked around for a place to hide it. She wanted time to think about all this before she shared anything with anyone else.

As she heard Violet noisily climbing the stairs, she pushed the bag and the metal box under her bed. She had forgotten to even look at the papers in the box, but then she didn't know much about legal papers. She would ask Ossie to go through them when he returned from Charleston. In the meantime she had to get downstairs and help with dinner.

She felt ashamed of herself for not having warmed the food by the time the others got back, and she apologized to Aunt Ida May.

"I'm sorry. I just got so involved in other things that I didn't realize it was time for y'all to be back from church," she told her aunt as they hurried to get everything on the table.

Logan and Roy offered to help, but Ida May had shooed them outside.

"Go take a walk or something," she told them. "We'll let you know when everything's ready."

They laughed and stepped out onto the porch where Violet, who had already changed out of her Sunday dress, was playing with the puppy and kitten.

"I'm just going to run up and check on Janie Belle and Aaron and see if they're ready for their dinner," Ida May said as she left the kitchen. "I'll be right back."

"I'll take up the cornbread," Lily called to her.

But instead, she ran to the back door and managed to attract Logan's attention without Roy being aware of her. Logan walked over to the door.

"I have to talk to you later. I've been to the house," Lily whispered. But then she saw Roy turn around and look at her, and she said loudly, "Why y'all come on back in and bring Violet with you if you don't mind. We'll eat as soon as Aunt Ida May comes back downstairs."

Logan frowned and gave Lily a hard look as they all came into the kitchen. Ida May came in from the hallway.

"They're not very hungry right now so I'll take something up later," Ida May said as she led the way into the dining room.

There wasn't much conversation at the table because there was lots of good food and everyone ate as if starving.

Lily tried to figure out how she could get the brocade bag down to her sewing room and have a chance to show the jewelry to Logan. She knew he wouldn't know anything about legal papers, so she wouldn't bother bringing the box down.

Accidentally the chance presented itself. Somehow Lily spilled a little coffee on her dress. She jumped up and asked to be excused to change dresses and put the dirty one to soak so it wouldn't stain.

"I'm sorry, but I'll be right back. Don't eat everything up," she teased as she hurried from the room.

Upstairs she removed the dress, put it to soak in the tub in her bathroom, and put on a fresh dress. Luckily the stained dress was an old one, just in case the coffee didn't come out.

Remembering the brocade bag, she bent and pulled it out from under her bed and hastily carried it down the steps to her sewing room, where she hid it in a cabinet. Then she returned to the table and smiled at Logan.

The problem now would be to get Logan away from the others but that, too, resolved itself easily. Roy had to return home as soon as he had eaten to attend to necessary chores, and Lily hurriedly helped Aunt Ida May clear the table of dirty dishes. The food itself was covered with another tablecloth and left on the table for supper.

When everything was done, Ida May told her, "I must take a tray up to Janie Belle and Aaron now. I might be a little while because I want to see if she's in the right mood for me to ask about taking that little bedroom for a playroom for Violet."

"That's fine," Lily said. "I wanted to ask Logan about a pair of his pants that I haven't done yet. I'm not sure how much he wants taken up."

"I'll be back soon," her aunt said after she had a tray ready.

As soon as Ida May left the kitchen, Lily hurriedly told Logan, who had been sitting at the far end of the room, "Come on to my sewing room. I want to show you something and ask about a pair of pants you gave me to hem."

Violet was on the back porch. Lily told her not to go out into the yard, and then she led Logan to her sewing room.

"You say you've been back to your father's house," Logan said as he followed her into the room.

"Yes, and I need to know whether it's one or two inches you want taken up on these pants," Lily said, hastily holding up a pair of work pants.

"About two inches. They're way too long," Logan replied.

Lily laid them down on the table and went to get the brocade bag from the cabinet. As she silently placed it on the sewing table, Logan watched.

"What's that?" he finally asked.

Lily grinned big and said, "My mother's jewelry! I told you it was in the house." She opened the bag and lifted up several pieces to show him.

Logan bent to look at the things and asked, "Are these real?"

"I have no idea, but I plan to take them to a jeweler and find out," Lily said. "And you'll never guess how I found them."

Logan shook his head in puzzlement as Lily related the events of that morning. "I just don't know what to think of Wilbur," she said.

"I told you the old man was dangerous. Even his own son must know it, knocking him out like that," Logan said as he scratched his head. "And you'd better hope the old man doesn't find out that you were in the house or that you have this stuff here. He'll make trouble over it. That's for sure."

"I'm not going to let anyone know I have these except for you, and the jeweler of course," Lily said.

"You took a big chance going over to that house by your-self," Logan reminded her. "Imagine what would have happened if the old man had found you and not Wilbur."

"I know. It scares me to think about it," Lily replied. She returned the pieces to the bag and fastened it.

"I told you I would go over there with you, remember?" Logan reminded her. "I know I'm not no kin, but I feel responsible for you. Please don't take such chances again."

"Thank you, Logan," Lily said as she placed the bag back in the cabinet. "I know I should have waited for you and I'm sorry. You're not blood kin, but I love you like an uncle. I always have."

At that moment Violet burst into the room. "Lily, my puppy ran away," she said. "I have to go get him."

"No," Lily said firmly as she and Logan started to leave the room. "I'll go with you to get him. You are not to go by yourself."

"You see there, Miss Lily," Logan said with a big grin.

"Your little sister is as headstrong as you. That one is going to have to be watched." He laughed.

Yes, Lily thought, *Violet was trying to do what she had done that morning—forget about authority and just go ahead with what she wanted.*

Chapter Twelve
Possibilities

Aunt Janie Belle had given permission for the play-room and Logan and Roy came to move the furni-ture out of the little bedroom to the attic on Monday morning.

Lily was eagerly awaiting the chance to ask Logan to go with her into town that afternoon to consult with the jeweler, and she caught him between trips to the attic.

"Will you go into town with me this afternoon?" she whispered to him. "I want to show the jeweler some of the jewelry and see what he thinks, whether it's real or not."

"Are you going to sell it?" Logan asked as they stood in the hallway after Roy and Ida May had gone to the attic with some pillows and things.

"Sell it?" Lily asked, frowning. "I had not even thought about that."

"It would give you a chance to get on your own two feet if it's worth much at all," Logan said.

"Well, I don't know," Lily said, wishing with all her heart she could keep the jewelry, but then her mother had said in her letter that if it were ever necessary Lily should go right ahead and sell it. "Maybe, maybe not. I'll have to do some hard thinking about it."

Ida May and Roy came down the steps and Logan quickly said, "Yes, I'll go into town with you if you want. I sure don't want you carrying that stuff around by yourself if it is real."

Lily gasped at the idea. She had not even thought about safety.

"I'll be ready right after dinner," she quickly told him. "And you know that you and Roy are invited to dinner with us."

"Yes, Aggie's in there concocting something right now," Logan said with a laugh.

They were finished emptying the room by the time Aggie had the meal on the table. She called them, and they all sat down in the kitchen to eat.

"Roy, would you please let me know just as soon as Ossie comes back from Charleston, or would you tell him I'd like to see him as soon as possible?" Lily told the foreman as they passed the potatoes.

"Sure will. May be a few days, never can tell how long he'll be gone, but soon as he gets in I'll pass the message," Roy promised.

"Lily, we need to make plans for the playroom, what we're going to put in there and everything," Aunt Ida May said as she buttered her bread.

"All right, Aunt Ida May. Tonight, maybe," Lily agreed. "After we eat, Logan is going into town and I'm going with him. I want to pick up a couple of things. Is there anything you need from town?"

"No, dear, not that I can think of, but you go right ahead when you finish your dinner. Aggie will be here all day, so I don't need any help to clear the table," her aunt said.

So when the meal was finished, Lily ran upstairs to change her dress, and then she and Logan went into Fountain Inn. Lily knew the jeweler's name but didn't really know the man. So when Logan pulled the cart up under a tree, she asked him to go inside with her.

Lily had not brought the whole bag of jewelry. She had dumped most of it out into another bag and left it under her bed. Logan's remark had made her self-conscious about safety.

There was no one in the shop when Lily and Logan entered. The little bell on the door had tinkled when they pushed the door open, and Mr. Stroupe came into the shop from the room at the back.

He was a tall, elderly man with thinning grey hair and wrinkled face. He smiled at them and asked, "What might I do for you today?" He looked directly at Lily and glanced at Logan.

"I have something I'd like to ask the worth of," Lily began as she pulled a necklace with what looked like rubies in it out of the bag and held it out to the man. "I have some more in here, too."

The man was surprised, took the necklace, got his magnifying glass, and examined it. Then he asked to see what else she had.

"Here are two different earrings," Lily said, handing them to him. "Of course I have both sets, but I only brought one of each."

"Yes, ma'am," Mr. Stroupe said as he quickly looked through his glass at the earring with a blue stone and the other one with a pearl.

He kept turning them over and over and looking and looking until Lily became impatient. *How long does it take to examine a piece of jewelry to see if it was real?* she wondered. She watched him closely.

"Well?" she finally said as she glanced up at Logan. He, too, was watching the man.

"I—I—uh—don't believe they're worth much," Mr. Stroupe mumbled as he picked up the necklace and examined it again. "I could probably give you a few dollars for these, provided you have the mates for the earrings, that is." He looked at her, and Lily looked up at Logan. She saw Logan shake his head.

"I don't want to sell them," she quickly said. "I only wanted to know how much they'd be worth if I should decide to sell them."

Mr. Stroupe quickly shoved the jewelry across the counter to her and said, "Then I have other things to do."

Lily was surprised at the man's attitude. She carefully returned the pieces to the brocade bag and said, "Thank you."

She and Logan left the shop. Outside, Logan frowned and said, "There was something strange about the way that man was acting. I'm glad that you said you didn't want to sell the jewelry."

"Well, this was a waste of time for you and me both," Lily said as they got back into the cart. "Logan, there are several jewelers in Greenville. Do you think we could go up there?"

Logan looked at her and smiled. "Not today. How about tomorrow morning?"

"That soon?" Lily said excitedly. "Thank you, Logan. Maybe we could catch the sheriff in his office while we're there and we could ask questions about Papa's death."

"That's exactly what I was thinking. You just be ready right after you have your breakfast tomorrow morning then," Logan told her.

That night Lily took all the jewelry out of the bag, carefully wiped each piece with a clean linen handkerchief, and returned each piece back to the bag.

She even dreamed about the jewelry. Someone was chasing her trying to snatch the bag, and the dream was so real she woke trembling in the middle of the night. She had to get up to be sure her mother's jewelry was all still in the bag under her bed.

The next morning, Lily put on one of her best dresses and hats after breakfast and was ready and waiting when Logan arrived. She had told Ida May she was going into Greenville and would try to catch up with the sheriff. She had bought some ribbon in Fountain Inn the day before so her reason for going wouldn't be just a lie, but she needed the ribbon anyway for the blue dress she planned to make for Violet for Christmas.

She and Logan went to two jewelers in Greenville, and both jewelers told Lily the jewels were real but would not say how much they were worth.

When they left the second shop, Lily asked Logan, "Is there anyone else here in Greenville we could ask about these?"

Logan scratched his head for a moment and said, "Seems like I heard tell of one of those Yankees coming to town and opening a shop. You could try him. I think we can find it."

They walked a little farther and found the shop. Greenville Jewelers was the name over the door, and Lily thought that was far from true if these people were not from here.

When Lily set the brocade bag on the counter, the man in the back came forward with a big smile. "And good morning. May I be of service?" he greeted her and he also nodded to Logan.

Lily was immediately impressed by the man's manners. She could tell from his accent that he was not a local man, but he sure had better manners than the other two jewelers.

"I have some jewelry here that I'd like to find out if it's real or not," Lily explained as she drew the necklace out of the bag and held it out.

The man glanced at the bag and at the necklace and then at Lily and said, "If I may be so bold, aren't you from Fountain Inn?"

Lily looked at him in surprise and said, "Well, yes, out in the country near Fountain Inn."

"Ah, Miss Masterson, I believe," the man continued with a big smile.

Lily was really surprised now and, when she glanced up at Logan, she could see he was, too.

"Yes, but how do you know so much about me?" she asked.

"I believe I met a relative of yours, Miss Ida May Masterson, at church a few weeks ago," the man replied as he reached for the necklace.

"And what is your name?" Lily asked.

"Oh, I do beg your pardon. My name is John Ridley," he replied as he got his glass and began examining the necklace.

Lily silently watched. She noticed Logan didn't take his eyes off the man. Was he suspicious of him?

Mr. Ridley straightened up, laid down his glass, and said, "You have a very valuable necklace here. Those are real stones, and flawless as far as I can tell."

Lily's eyes grew big and she quickly pulled out the two earrings.

"What about these?" she asked.

Mr. Ridley quickly examined them and said, "More real stones. Were you wanting to sell these pieces?"

Lily quickly glanced at Logan who slightly shook his head, and she said, "Not at the present, but I might later. I wanted to see if they were real and how much I might be able to get for them."

"Then they are not yours?" Mr. Ridley asked.

"Oh, yes, they're mine. I inherited them, among other things," she hastily explained. "How much would you be willing to pay for them if I sold them?"

Mr. Ridley thought for a moment, did some figuring on a piece of paper, and then handed it to her. He watched as she read the figures.

"That much?" she said with a gasp, and handed the paper to Logan, who frowned as he read it.

"Then if you are offering that much for these pieces, they must be worth a lot more, because you'd have to make a profit in order to stay in business," Logan spoke for the first time.

"Well, yes, they are worth more, a little more," Mr. Ridley said. "But you see, in this case I know of Miss Masterson and I know what hard luck she has had since her father died."

"You knew my father?" Lily quickly asked.

"No, but he was well-known, and I have heard about the misfortunes you have had. I'd be glad to try to help a little by giving you a good price for the jewelry," he explained.

"Thank you," Lily said, reaching for the jewelry. "I appreciate your kindness, but I am not absolutely sure I want to sell any of this right now. However, I will come back if I do." She closed the brocade bag and fastened it. "I thank you very much."

"Yes, Mr. Ridley, we appreciate your kindness and we may return," Logan added.

"If you don't sell, please come back by to see me when you come to Greenville again," Mr. Ridley told Logan.

"Will do," Logan replied.

As they went outside, Lily said, "I can't believe that. My mother must have been awfully rich to own stuff like this."

"Don't forget you said she inherited some or most of it, remember," Logan reminded her. "Now, are we on the trail of that sheriff again?" He grinned.

"Oh, yes, let's see if he's in," Lily agreed.

They went back to Logan's cart and rode to the courthouse yard under the trees.

But when they went to the office of the sheriff, he was not there. And no one seemed to know where the sheriff was. Lily was carrying the brocade bag, afraid to put it down anywhere.

"Well, I just don't believe he ever stays in his office, do you?" Lily said with disappointment.

"I know we have a sheriff, but I don't ever see him," Logan agreed.

"I have an idea," Lily said as they started to the front door. "Ossie told me we could come to the courthouse and look up records to see if my father owned any other property. Do we have time to do that?"

"Well, yes, if you know where to go or what to do," Logan agreed. "That's something I don't know anything about."

"I'll ask at the window over there," Lily said.

The woman at the window was glad to explain exactly where the records were and how one would go about searching them. The office for land records was on the second floor.

Once they were in the land office Lily gave her brocade bag to Logan for safekeeping while she wrestled with the huge volumes of handwritten real estate records.

"If you would hold on to the bag for me, it would be

easier to do this," she explained as she took down a heavy volume from the shelf and opened it.

"Sure will," Logan said as he watched her, and he took the bag from her hand.

"Let's see, that woman said to look in the index for the name of the landowner and it will give the volume and page number for the property," Lily said as she ran her forefinger down the columns of names. Then excitedly she said, "Here's my father's name, Charles Masterson."

Logan looked over her shoulder as she added, "And according to this, I should look in Volume D, page 333, for the property listing."

She quickly returned the volume to the shelf, took down the one marked D, and turned to page 333.

"Well, this is our house we lived in," she said. She looked up at Logan and said, "And this is the only reference by my father's name in the index. So I suppose he didn't own anything else."

"Could be he owned something a long time ago and sold it, couldn't it?" Logan asked.

"Well, I suppose, but that would take a long time for me to hunt up that kind of record, and I think we'd better be going home," Lily said, returning the volume to the shelf. "I know you have other things to do, and I should be home to keep an eye on Violet so Aunt Ida May won't have her hands full."

"We can come back another day, and maybe then we can catch up with that sheriff," Logan told her as he handed her the brocade bag.

"Yes, he's just got to be in his office sometime or other," Lily said as they left the building.

On the way home, Logan was driving the cart along and asked, "So you're not going to sell any of your mother's jewelry?"

"I don't really want to. I know she said in her letter I should if necessary, but I don't really want to part with it," Lily answered as she held the brocade bag in her lap.

"I was just thinking you could be independent of your aunt if you sold just what you've got in that bag," Logan told her. "You could have your own place and get your sewing business going."

"I know, but I'll have to do some hard thinking about it first," Lily said.

She was torn between the idea of her freedom from dependence on relatives and the sentimental value of the jewels. She would discuss this with Ossie. He was a businessman. He could advise her.

Chapter Thirteen
What to Do Now?

L ily didn't have much time to think about the decision she must make. The next morning as soon as breakfast was finished, she rushed to her room and dressed to go to Greenville with Logan. She was coming back down the staircase when she heard a knock on the front door. As she came to the bottom of the steps she saw Aunt Ida May coming up the hallway to answer it. It couldn't be Logan at the front door. He, and everyone else she knew, always came to the back door.

"Good morning, sheriff," Lily heard her aunt say as she opened the door.

Lily stopped on the bottom step. She saw a tall heavyset man with grey curly hair, a grey mustache, and deep-set dark eyes standing on the front porch outside the door. She could not remember ever having seen the sheriff, and she decided now that he looked large enough to do his job.

"I would like to see Miss Lily Masterson," he told Aunt Ida May.

Her aunt stepped back and motioned to him as she said,

"Of course, come right in, sheriff. If you'll have a seat in the parlor over there, I'll get her." She indicated a room to her left as the sheriff hung his hat on the hall tree.

"I'm right here, Aunt Ida May," Lily said as her aunt turned and saw her. Lily stepped forward as she greeted the man, "I'm Lily Masterson, sheriff."

"Let's all go into the parlor," Ida May said. She ushered the man and Lily into the room. "Have a seat, sheriff."

The big man sat on the edge of a chair as Lily followed Ida May to the settee.

The sheriff seemed to be hesitating to speak. Lily spoke up. "I'm glad we're finally able to meet and talk," she said.

He suddenly stood up and said, as he pulled a paper from his pocket, "I'm John Meadows, sheriff for Greenville County, and I'm here to take the stolen jewelry you've been going around trying to sell, Miss Lily Masterson."

Lily jumped up, gasping in alarm. Ida May quickly rose to her feet.

"What?" Lily exclaimed, shaking from head to toe with anger. "What are you talking about?"

She remained standing in the middle of the floor.

"I said you have been trying to sell stolen jewelry, and I have a paper here demanding that you turn the stuff over to me," he continued, shaking the paper in his hand.

"Now, you just wait a minute, sheriff," Lily said angrily. "I have not stolen any jewelry or anything. The jewelry I have shown to several jewelers belonged to my mother and was passed down to me when she died. I *own* that jewelry."

"That's not what I've been told," the sheriff retorted.

Ida May spoke up. "She is telling you the truth, sheriff. She inherited that jewelry from her mother," she said, glancing questioningly at Lily.

"Just what is going on here in my house?" Aunt Janie Belle suddenly appeared in the doorway, shouting at the man. "How dare you accuse my niece of stealing! Please leave my house immediately. Right now!"

The man looked at her with his mouth open. It was plain to see he was afraid of Janie Belle's wrath.

"But I have a paper here that says your niece stole that jewelry out of the house that was sold for taxes," the sheriff insisted.

Lily gasped in surprise. Had Wilbur tricked her? If so, why? Just what was going on? And she was aware that both her aunts seemed puzzled and were staring at her.

"Just who is this who claims I have stolen jewelry?" Lily demanded.

The man looked at the paper and said, "The complaint is signed by Weyman Braddock, attorney for Mr. Whitaker who bought the house."

Lily, Ida May, and Janie Belle looked at each other. The old man Whitaker was still after her.

"Well, you can tell Mr. Whitaker we'll see him in court. Now, please leave my premises," Janie Belle angrily told him, still standing near the doorway. "And don't come back. Any sheriff who can't investigate my brother's death is not welcome in my home. Now, go."

Lily immediately had a question of her own. "When can I see you to talk about my father's death? No one believes he was killed while shoeing a horse. He was too much of an expert for that," she said. "And I want the case reopened and thoroughly investigated."

The man looked at her, hastily picked up his hat, and headed for the door. "That case is closed," he said. "There is nothing more to discuss regarding it."

The sheriff went out into the hallway, and Ida May opened the front door to wait for him to leave.

As he looked back, he said, "You know you people have to abide by the law. We'll see to that." He ran down the front steps toward his horse tethered at the mounting block.

Ida May closed the door, and the three women looked at each other there in the hallway.

"Now, Lily, I think you owe us an explanation," Aunt Janie Belle told her. "We defended you, but we don't know exactly what we were defending."

Lily rushed to embrace Aunt Janie Belle. If it were not for her cane, Lily's aunt would have lost her balance.

"Aunt Janie Belle, I'm sorry. I'll explain everything," she told the lady who looked unsure about what was going on.

"Let's go to the kitchen. The coffeepot is on the stove," Ida May urged them.

As they walked down the hallway toward the kitchen, Lily suddenly remembered she was supposed to go to Greenville with Logan.

"I wonder what's happened to Logan," Lily said, looking around the warm kitchen. "He should have been here by now. We're supposed to go to Greenville and do some shopping," she told Aunt Janie Belle.

And at that very moment Logan came rushing through the back door without even knocking. He looked worried as he entered the kitchen.

"What's goin' on? Anything you need help on?" he asked. He tossed his hat on the peg by the door and looked at the three women. "I just met the sheriff in the driveway, and something had him fit to be tied."

"Sit down, Logan. I've got to explain some things," Lily told him. She grabbed cups and saucers from the cupboard and brought them to the table where Aunt Janie Belle had already taken a chair.

"Yes, sit down, Logan. Lily will be ready to go in a few minutes, I'm sure," Janie Belle told him.

After Lily helped Aunt Ida May fill the coffee cups and everyone was served, Lily began her story.

"First of all, I have to apologize to you, Aunt Janie Belle, and you, Aunt Ida May," Lily began as she looked around the table. "I apologize with all my heart, but I was so wrapped up in my own feelings, I guess I didn't think about my obligations to my two aunts."

"Nonsense, child, you are not under obligation to us," Aunt Janie Belle cut in. "Just get on with the explanation about this jewelry."

"Yes, ma'am," Lily said meekly. She was glad to know Aunt Janie Belle felt that way. She looked at Logan and said, "To begin with, Logan, the sheriff says Mr. Whitaker claims I stole my mother's jewelry from our house that he bought."

"What?" Logan practically shouted as he looked around the table. "That sorry scoundrel! Just let me—"

"No, Logan, first let me explain to my aunts about the jewelry," Lily quickly interrupted him. Then looking at the ladies, she said, "When I was going through Papa's desk in the attic the other day, I found this letter my mother had written to him—"

Janie Belle interrupted. "A letter your mother wrote to your father?" she asked.

"Yes, ma'am," Lily said. "It was dated the year before she died, on her birthday." Her voice trembled with emotion, and she drew a deep breath and continued. "She wrote in the letter that she wanted me to have all her jewelry and—"

Janie Belle interrupted again. "So that's why you asked us so many questions about jewelry," she said. "Lily, dear, why didn't you just tell us straightforth what you wanted to know?"

"And you found the jewelry in your father's house?" Ida May added.

Lily looked from one aunt to the other and replied, "Aunt Janie Belle, the letter was such a shock to find, and for the time being I felt it was too personal to share. And I did find my mother's jewelry in a secret hiding place in our house."

"Well, do tell us about the secret hiding place," Aunt Janie Belle said. "I was raised in that house, you know, and I never did know anything about a secret hiding place."

Lily smiled at her as she stood up and said, "First, let me run upstairs and bring the jewelry down here for y'all to see. I'll be right back." She hurried from the room.

She pulled the brocade bag from under her bed and rushed back down to the kitchen. Her aunts were going to be interested in seeing the broken pearl necklace that they had told her about.

Lily brought the bag to the table, turned it upside down, and allowed the jewelry to slowly slide out. Her aunts watched in surprise. Logan had not seen all of it so he also leaned forward to look.

"My goodness, child!" Aunt Ida May exclaimed. "Do you mean to say all this belonged to your mother?"

"Yes, ma'am," Lily said as she explained how she had found the jewelry in her father's house that day. She removed the broken necklace last. "And here are the pearls y'all remember seeing her wear." She handed them to Aunt Janie Belle next to her.

"Yes, these are the ones, I'm sure," she said as she carefully handled the necklace. "Don't you think, Ida May?" She passed it on to Ida May.

"They certainly were your mother's. You see, I told you I thought there were three strands and that one strand broke," Ida May agreed.

Lily looked at Logan and asked, "Do you remember seeing my mother wear any of this?"

"Why, I sure did see her decked out in all this finery," Logan said as he examined the pearls. "Now that you have it all spread out here, my memory comes back. There are the pearl earrings she wore." He indicated the matching earrings.

"And, Aunt Janie Belle and Aunt Ida May, I took these pieces to the jewelers in Greenville," Lily said, picking up the necklace and two of the earrings. "And the man, his name is Mr. John Ridley, told me they were real and worth a lot of money."

"My word, child!" Ida May exclaimed and caught her breath. "But you are not planning on selling your mother's jewelry, are you?"

"I'm not sure," Lily said, glancing at both aunts. "I'll have to think about it."

Ida May cleared her throat and said, "But you know, you probably have jewelry worth enough here to buy back your father's house."

Lily gasped. She looked at her two aunts. "Why, I had not even thought of that," she finally said. Then turning to Logan, she asked, "Do you think that would be possible?"

"Maybe, maybe not," he said. "Unless you wanted to take all this stuff into Greenville and ask Mr. Ridley what the total would be there's no way to tell."

"Lily, I've told you before," Janie Belle said as she laid down a diamond brooch. "Don't count on ever getting your property back. That Mr. Whitaker is not going to sell it cheap, especially now with his accusations against you. And this Mr. Ridley you're talking about must have told him you had the jewelry."

Lily looked at Logan and said, "Somehow I trusted Mr. Ridley, didn't you? I didn't trust the jeweler here in Fountain Inn because he acted so strange. Not only that, no one knew I had found the jewelry except Wilbur Whitaker. Do you think he is the cause of all this trouble with the sheriff?"

"He could be, but I hardly think so. After all, he had found the hidin' place and took the jewelry out of it and gave it to you," Logan said. "I would think the man in the Fountain Inn store told him. He seemed suspicious to me. He's also new in town and we don't know anything about him. He could be connected with Whitaker, and who knows what all Whitaker is involved in."

Lily's mind quickly picked up on that remark. "Like the death of my father," she said thoughtfully.

"Lily, now don't start imagining things like that. Keep your thoughts on the present. We've got to clear up this problem with the jewelry," Aunt Janie Belle told her. "Did you take the jewelry anywhere else?"

"We started with the store in Fountain Inn and then when we went to Greenville we asked at two other jewelers before we talked to Mr. Ridley at the last store," Lily explained. One piece of her mind was still considering the suspicions that Logan had of Mr. Stroupe, the Fountain Inn jeweler.

"Well, whoever the culprit is, it won't do him a bit of good," Aunt Janie Belle was saying, as Lily came back to the present. "It's plain that all this belonged to your mother and that you are the legal owner now, no matter what that Mr. Whitaker says."

"And if that Whitaker man causes trouble over this, I'd say you would be able to countersue," Logan told Lily. "After all, I've been with the family for many a year, and I have never heard of any Masterson bein' accused of dishonesty in any way. Why, this is enough to make your Grandpa Tad turn over in his grave."

Lily smiled at the old man and said, "I only want to clear my name. And I want that man to leave me alone."

"I understand, dear," Aunt Janie Belle said. Then looking at Logan she asked, "Do you have time to wait until I can write a quick letter to my lawyer in Greenville? And maybe you could deliver it to him for me while you're there instead of waiting for the slow mail."

"Of course, Miss Janie Belle," Logan agreed. "That's a fine thing you're doing for Miss Lily. I'll be glad to take it straight to the man as soon as we get in town."

Aunt Janie Belle rose, and when the others started to rise, she stopped them, saying, "Now y'all just sit still. I'll go up to my rooms and consult with Aaron. He's reading by the fire up there. And I'll be back shortly with the letter."

Everyone sat back down and Aunt Janie Belle left the room.

"What would I do without you and Aunt Janie Belle and Logan?" Lily said with a sigh.

"Don't worry about a thing, child. You know your Aunt Janie Belle well enough to know she will take care of everything," Ida May told her. "And if you think of anything at all I can do to help, please let me know at once."

"That goes for me, too," Logan added. "Stuff like this makes you want to put a gate on the town and not let any outsiders in. We don't need these strangers comin' in here and causin' trouble like this. As far as I'm concerned they can all go back to where they came from."

Lily smiled at him and said, "But that gate would have kept my mother from ever coming here. Remember, she was a foreigner."

Logan seemed embarrassed as he admitted, "Well, I suppose you're right. And your mother was a good lady. Everyone liked her."

"Yes, she was," Ida May agreed. Changing the subject, she asked, "Since y'all are going into Greenville, would you mind picking up a few items for me?"

"Of course, we will, Aunt Ida May. You just make a list of whatever you want, and we'll get it," Lily said.

"Well, you will be able to get what I need at the Red Hot Racket, and you're going there anyway," Ida May said as she rose and walked over to the sewing machine and opened a drawer. "I'm almost out of green embroidery thread for that pillow top I'm making. I'll give you a sample since I don't remember the number, but they'll know what it is at that store." She returned to the table and handed Lily a short strand of green thread.

"How many do you need?" Lily asked, taking the thread.

"That particular color is good on lots of other things so I'd say get about six of the small hanks. I can work better with the smaller hanks," Ida May replied. She sat back down at the table. "And while I think of it, Lily, you need to put the material for that dress for me on my charge account there."

"Oh, goodness, I had not even thought of money," Lily said. "I suppose I was planning on putting it on Papa's account. The man had told me he would continue the charges for me. And now that I will be able to get some money of my own, if I sell some of the jewelry, I can keep the charge account."

"No, I insist you put the material and anything that you need for now on my account, Lily," Ida May firmly told her. "I don't want you rushing into parting with any of your mother's jewelry."

"Well," Lily reluctantly agreed. "But I will settle up with you later."

Aunt Janie Bell came back into the kitchen. She went straight to Logan and handed him a long white sealed envelope. "I'd greatly appreciate it if you will just hand this to Mr. Anderson himself," she said as Logan rose to accept the envelope. "And if you will, please tell him that he will have to come out here to consult with us. I'm just not in shape to make that tiresome trip to Greenville right now."

"Yes, ma'am, will do," Logan said. He tucked the envelope in his hip pocket.

"I'll be ready to leave as soon as I run upstairs and get my hat," Lily said. She stood up, put the jewelry back into the brocade bag, and started toward the hall door.

"We may be gone a while, Miss Lily, because I need to go into Fountain Inn on the way and drop an order off at the feed store for Roy," Logan told her.

"That's all right," Lily called to him as she left the room.

Once upstairs she shoved the bag under her bed and grabbed her hat. Quickly looking into the mirror on her dresser, she put the hat on her head and stuck a large hatpin through it to hold it in place.

In the back of her mind she felt that she did look presentable to visit Aunt Janie Belle's lawyer. She had made the suit she wore, and it was a perfect fit. Picking up her small purse, she put the green thread sample inside, took her gloves from the bureau and hurried back downstairs.

Lily felt confident that with Aunt Janie Belle behind her everything would turn out all right. She was grateful for both her aunts' support and Logan's loyalty. She hurried down the hallway.

When she reached the kitchen, Aunt Janie Belle had left the room. Aunt Ida May and Logan were seated at the table again, and they rose when she entered the room.

"Now, Lily, don't worry about rushing back. I'll be here when Violet gets home from school and will look after her. You and Logan should take time to enjoy your trip. The only thing I'd ask is that you get home before dark. I'll have supper waiting," Ida May told her. "And Logan has promised to eat with us."

Lily smiled as she looked at the two. She felt there was an attraction between Aunt Ida May and Logan, and she secretly hoped it would materialize into something good.

"Thanks, Aunt Ida May," Lily said as she and Logan left the room.

The autumn sun was shining and the day was warm. They rode in Logan's open cart and made the stop in Fountain Inn.

The feed store was near the depot, and Lily saw and heard the train coming down the track. Trains always excited her, and she asked Logan, "Could we slow down and watch the train stop?" She grinned.

Logan grinned back. "I love trains, too," he said, slowing the cart to a stop in front of the passenger building. "Might as well stop here anyway. You just watch the train come in, and I'll step down to the feed store."

He looped the reins over a hitching post and jumped down.

Lily held her hand out and said, "Me, too. I'll walk around here while you go to the feed store."

Logan assisted her down. He went on toward the store, and Lily walked around the building to see the train as it came to a stop behind the platform.

Lily stood there watching as the passengers left the train. Some of them went into the waiting room, and others walked toward the road. She was turning to go back to the road when she suddenly heard her name called.

"Lily, Lily!" a male voice called.

Lily turned and saw Ossie hurrying from the train to catch up with her. She was surprised that he had returned so soon from Charleston.

When he had caught up with her, Ossie laughed and said, "This is a nice surprise, you meeting me at the train."

Lily laughed also and said, "Well, I didn't exactly come to meet you. I'm with Logan, and he's gone to the feed store to place an order for Roy. Then we're going to Greenville."

"Well, anyhow, it's a pleasant encounter," Ossie said, pushing his spectacles up on his nose. "And if I may ask, what are you going to Greenville for?"

Lily could hardly talk fast enough to bring Ossie up to date on her affairs. He listened carefully to every word before saying anything. She told him about the jewelry, the sheriff's visit, and everything else she could think of.

"So many things have just suddenly popped up," she said, at last running out of breath.

"I'm just flabbergasted that Whitaker would have the nerve to accuse you of something like that," Ossie said. "And I'm not too sure there isn't something underhanded about his son, Wilbur."

Logan came back and joined them standing there by the cart. After greeting each other, Logan said, "Why don't you just run to Greenville and back with us? You'd have more time to talk."

Ossie looked at Lily and asked, "Would you like that?"

"Oh, of course, Ossie, but be prepared. I'll talk your ears off on the way."

So, after seeing to his luggage, Ossie joined them in the cart, and they continued their journey to Greenville.

Chapter Fourteen
Bringing It All Together

They went to the lawyer's office first. Logan parked the cart nearby, and the three of them walked to the two-story building near the courthouse on Main Street in Greenville.

As Logan led the way he told Lily, "I'm afraid you'll have to go up some outside steps to get to Mr. Anderson's office. I suppose that's why Miss Janie Belle doesn't make visits here and insists that he come out to the house."

They stopped in front of the drugstore, which was on street level, and Lily looked up at the stairs on the side of the building.

"That's not a problem with me, long as you and Ossie go ahead of me," Lily said with a little laugh. "That way I can go as slow as I want."

"Sure you don't want me to stay behind in case you trip or something?" Ossie asked as they walked on toward the steps.

"No, thank you, Ossie," Lily replied as she gathered up her long skirts and waved them ahead of her. At the top she shook out her skirts and laughed. "You see, I made it in one whole piece."

"Thank goodness," Ossie replied.

Logan grinned and said, "I remember how rough you played when you were a child, climbing trees, jumping off the barn roof, and all that. I wasn't worried."

Lily felt her face growing warm to be reminded of those escapades. She was sixteen now and trying to act like a lady. "Please don't remind me!"

Logan led the way into the building's second story and down the short hallway to a door with a frosted glass in the upper half lettered GEORGE W. ANDERSON & SON, ATTORNEYS-AT-LAW, with smaller letters "Come in" down in the left bottom corner just above the brass doorknob. He took the letter from his hip pocket and pushed the door open.

Lily followed with Ossie behind her. She looked around. They were in a small room with a brocade-covered settee and two upholstered chairs. A young man came from the inner room to greet them. He was short and dark and wore spectacles.

"I have a letter here to deliver to Mr. George Anderson from Mrs. Janie Belle Woods," Logan said, looking down at the envelope in his hands.

The man reached for it as he said, "I am William Attley, Mr. Anderson's law clerk. I'll give it to him. He's not in right now."

Logan moved back a step or two and held onto the envelope. "I'm sorry, fella, but Mrs. Janie Belle directed me to give this personally to Mr. Anderson. When will he be in?"

"He's in court today," William Attley explained as he straightened up. "I have no idea as to when court will let out. I'm sorry."

"We have other errands so we'll jes' check back after while," Logan replied.

"I'll tell him you were here if he returns in the meantime," William Attley said.

Logan led the way out of the building and down the outside stairs. At the bottom he said, "Let's jes' go get that dress cloth for Miss Ida May and then check back here again."

"All right," Lily agreed.

"Whatever y'all wish to do. I'm just following," Ossie told them.

The three walked up Main Street to the store with the sign RED HOT RACKET hanging over the sidewalk and went inside.

Lily had been in the dry goods store once before, but she still stared around the inside. The store sold everything from washtubs to cheap jewelry. She walked across the creaky wooden floors and examined the merchandise displayed on every counter and finally came back to the dry goods counter with its stacks and stacks of satin, silk, voile, cotton, and muslin fabrics.

She removed her gloves. "I know I told Aunt Ida May I would get blue, but I really think this pink silk would look prettier on her," she said, running her fingers across the soft fabric. Looking at Ossie and Logan, she asked, "What do you men think?"

"Fine," Logan agreed.

"Pink for your Aunt Ida May?" Ossie questioned her.

"I'm sorry, Ossie, but I forgot to tell you that I talked Aunt Ida May into letting me make her a bright dress of some kind and replace the black ones she wears all the time," Lily explained.

"Good for you!" Ossie exclaimed with a smile. "Yes, the pink would look nice with her dark hair and eyes."

Lily purchased enough yardage to make her aunt a dress,

with all the ribbons, lace, and thread she needed, and then picked out the green embroidery thread for Aunt Ida May.

As soon as she was finished Logan and Ossie each took part of the packages, and they walked back down the street to check on Mr. Anderson.

When they entered the offices this time, they were greeted by a tall, handsome young man with a thin mustache and blond curly hair. His blue eyes smiled as he greeted them.

"Good morning, I know who you are. I'm George Anderson, Jr.," he said, shaking hands with all three. "William told me you all had been in and would return. My father has just come in. I'll tell him you're here. Please be seated."

As the three sat down, George, Jr., disappeared into the inner offices. Lily was silent, thinking about the young man. He had a nice smile and seemed to be very courteous. She had never seen him before, although her father had had the same attorney, his father, for something one time, she couldn't remember what.

In a few minutes a tall, distinguished-looking older man appeared in the doorway and introduced himself as George W. Anderson, Sr.

"I understand you have a letter for me from Mrs. Janie Belle Woods," he said, looking at Logan.

"Yes, sir, I'm Logan Garrett, and I had always worked for the Mastersons until Mr. Charlie passed away," Logan explained, handing him the envelope.

"Yes, sir, I believe I've met you before," Mr. Anderson said as he accepted the envelope. "Now if you will all excuse me, I'll withdraw into my office and see what Mrs. Woods has sent me. I'll rejoin you shortly if you would please wait."

"Yes, sir," Lily said as she sat back down.

"We'll be right here," Logan told him as he and Ossie sat on the settee.

"He and his son both seem to be courteous and friendly," Lily remarked as they waited.

"They make enough money off people to afford to be courteous and friendly," Ossie joked.

"Yes, but lawyers are a necessity sometimes," Logan said.

"I suppose Aunt Janie Belle wrote to ask him to represent me to get the mess settled about the jewelry," Lily remarked.

When Mr. Anderson appeared in the doorway shortly after that, he spoke directly to her. He said, "I won't write a reply if you would please tell your aunt, Mrs. Woods, that I will be out to consult with her tomorrow morning. And we need to have you present also, Miss Lily."

"Yes, sir, I'll be there, and I'll tell her," Lily replied as she rose. Ossie and Logan stood up, too.

When they arrived at Janie Belle's house later that day, Lily delivered the message and Janie Belle seemed relieved.

"Just be sure you are available tomorrow morning, dear," she told Lily.

"Don't worry," Lily said. "I'll be here."

When morning came, George Anderson knocked on Janie Belle's front door. He had brought his son with him. The two aunts, Uncle Aaron, and Lily went into the parlor with them to talk.

Mr. Anderson read the letter Lily had from her mother to her father about the jewelry. Lily explained how she found the jewelry, and that Whitaker's own son had given everything to her. And he looked at the collection in the brocade bag.

"This man Whitaker doesn't have a leg to stand on," Mr. Anderson said.

"That's what I was hoping you would say," Aunt Janie Belle told him.

"What about trespassing?" Uncle Aaron asked.

"Of course, she was trespassing, but I think if we threaten him with having made false accusations against Miss Masterson, he'll have sense enough not to pursue that charge," George Anderson replied.

"Do you think this will go to court?" Aunt Janie Belle asked.

"Well," Mr. Anderson said thoughtfully, "I don't know the man, but I've heard a lot about him—and nothing good I might say—so I'd say we'd better be prepared."

Lily was silent as the adults discussed the matter. She listened and constantly glanced under her eyelashes at George, Jr., who seemed to be intent on the discussion. He was awfully good-looking, and he did have a nice personality, she decided.

Then she was brought back to the present when Mr. Anderson said, "I'm sorry, Mrs. Woods, but I have so many commitments ahead of me in the near future, it may be necessary for George, Jr., here to represent Miss Lily in this matter."

Lily quickly looked at the older man and then at his son who was now smiling at her. She averted her gaze to her older aunt.

"Well, I certainly want to be sure Lily has proper legal counsel if we do have to go to court," Aunt Janie Belle was saying. "I suppose if George, Jr., needs help, you can assist him on the case."

"Oh, yes, ma'am," Mr. Anderson said. "Of course, I will. I will give him guidance and advice on everything. George, Jr., has been in the business now for more than two years, and we think he's doing pretty good, even if he is my son." He looked at George, Jr., with a big smile.

"All right then," Aunt Janie Belle replied. "The next move is up to Mr. Whitaker. I'll let you know if we hear further from him."

"And I thank you, ma'am, and Mr. Woods, Miss Masterson," Mr. Anderson said as he rose.

Lily didn't have long to wait before Mr. Whitaker's lawyer had a summons served on her to appear in court. Mr. Anderson had arranged for the paper to be delivered to his office, and George, Jr., brought it out to the Woodses' home.

George, Jr., was right. A few days later Lily had to appear in court. Everyone—Ossie, Roy, Logan, Aunt Ida May, Aunt Janie Belle, and Uncle Aaron—was there in support.

Lily was still so angry with Mr. Whitaker that she had little trouble overcoming her nervousness in the courtroom. She told the judge exactly what had happened. Mr. Anderson had already presented the letter her mother had written, and Wilbur was sitting in the back of the room.

"I am not guilty of stealing anything, your honor," Lily told the judge.

"And we would like to have the whole matter dismissed," George, Jr., told the judge when it was his turn to speak.

But Mr. Whitaker, angry with the way things were going, jumped from his seat and shouted, "I want something done about this. I am not willing to have this dismissed. I saw Lily Masterson with my own two eyes in my house before someone knocked me out. After I came to, I saw the secret place opened, and when I investigated, I found the inner door. I know the jewelry was in there, and I want her prosecuted."

The judge tapped on his podium. "Please, Mr. Whitaker, let's stay in order," he said.

At that moment Lily saw Wilbur hurrying down the aisle to stand before the judge. He stood there without speaking until the judge asked, "And what might you want, Mr. Wilbur Whitaker?"

"Your honor, I want to clear the name of Miss Lily Masterson," he said. "Every word she has spoken has been the truth. I was there. I had already found the jewelry in that hiding place, and I realized it belonged to her. I had tried several times, without any luck, to make contact with her and advise her of this, but that day I happened to find her in the house. I knocked my father out to keep him from catching her claiming her own property because I knew he would take it. I—"

Mr. Whitaker had jumped up again and interrupted, "You knocked me out? Why, I—"

The judge beat furiously with his gavel and said in a loud voice, "This court will be in order. Now, Mr. Whitaker, please be seated so I can see what your son has to say. Be seated or I'll hold you in contempt of court."

Lily glanced at the man and saw him reluctantly sit back down, all the time mumbling to himself.

"Now, young man, please continue," the judge told Wilbur.

"Lily Masterson is not guilty of anything, except claiming her own property," Wilbur said.

The judge recessed the hearing. He went into his private chambers to consider the odd turn of the case. When he reconvened the hearing he said, "I find no truth in the charges. The case is hereby dismissed."

Mr. Whitaker immediately jumped up, yelling, "I'll get her for trespassing. She's guilty of that."

The hearing over, George, Jr., stepped over to Mr. Whitaker, and Lily could hear him say, "Mr. Whitaker, if you wish to press trespassing charges, we will press charges of false accusations."

Mr. Whitaker was at a loss for words. He shook his head without a reply and left the courtroom. No one expected to hear much from him again.

Lily felt a load lifted off her shoulders. As everyone was leaving the courtroom, George, Jr., came to speak to her.

"I think it's all done and over with," he said, smiling.

"Thank you. I appreciate everything," she said. And then without even thinking she said, "You know there was a metal box full of legal papers in the hiding place with the jewelry. Would you be interested in going through them for me?"

"A metal box full of legal papers? That's something I'd like to get my teeth into. I'll contact you one day real soon."

On the way back to Aunt Janie Belle's house, her aunt had Logan, who was driving her rig, stop to check the mailbox before turning into the driveway.

Logan stepped down, opened the box, and pulled out a letter. He brought it back to Lily and said, "Looks like a letter from some foreign country."

"A letter from Aunt Emma!" she exclaimed.

As soon as everyone was in Aunt Janie Belle's kitchen and Aunt Ida May was putting on a pot of coffee, Lily stood in the middle of the floor and opened the letter. Everyone was seated around the kitchen table.

Silently reading at first, Lily suddenly gasped and said, "Listen to this, all of you. Aunt Emma says, 'How many times do I have to tell you that you have a home here? You must come at once and see about it. The executors have said it will be necessary for you and Violet to live in it until Violet comes of age, at which time she will inherit the home.' This is what my mother was writing about in her letter, that she had provided for Violet. Of all things!"

"But what are you going to do about it, dear? Your Aunt Emma says you have to live in it until Violet comes of age," Aunt Janie Belle asked.

Ossie, Logan, and Ida May had all stopped to listen.

Lily suddenly felt let down. She couldn't live in England for all those years until Violet was grown. Yes, what was she going to do about it?

"I would suggest you write to your Aunt Emma and get more details about this house," Ossie told her.

"And we certainly don't want you to go live in England," Aunt Janie Belle said.

"No, we don't," Ida May agreed. "You belong here with your people."

"Miss Lily, it's a long way to England. I don't think I'd be able to come visit, and I sure would miss you and Violet," Logan added.

"So many things keep happening," Lily said with a sigh as she sat down at the table with the others. "It's so confusing."

"It's not confusing at all, dear," Aunt Janie Belle told her. "We want you here with us."

"There may be something you can do about this house without even going to England," Ossie said. "Write to your Aunt Emma and ask lots of questions."

Lily blew out her breath and said, "I haven't even made my mind up yet about what I'll do with the jewelry. And now this."

"We're all here to help and advise you, Lily," Aunt Janie Belle told her. "And you don't have to rush about anything. Just take your time."

"Yes, I will have to take some time to decide about all

this," Lily agreed. "And I'll write to Aunt Emma before I go to bed tonight."

There were possibilities now. Violet owned a home in England and Lily possessed a fortune in jewelry. And the decision about her future could wait for now.

Are you a member of the Lily fan club? If not, write,

Lily's Fan Club
P. O. Box 5972
Greenville, S.C. 29606